TURMOIL IN UNIVERSES

Alex Tanen, a small-time night club magician, suddenly wins a $1,000,000 sweepstakes. He tries to collect—and is soon battling alligators, monster Constructs, minotaurs . . . because Alex's "prize" is a lure to another world.

Easy Gordon—the American mercenary adventurer who traveled Glory Road, the path between alternate universes—needs his old war buddy Alex's help to stop a psychopathic sadist whose sorcerous powers threaten the Twenty Universes. Alex must survive dragons, lightning creatures, antigravity zones, ray-gun wielding knights on flying horses to get to the performance of his life, before an evil audience of one. If Alex gets stagefright, the cosmos is doomed. But Alex Tanen's magic is illusion . . .

His enemy's tricks are *real* . . .

CROSSROADS™ ADVENTURES are authorized interactive novels compatible with any role-playing game. Constructed by the masters of modern gaming, CROSSROADS™ feature complete rules, *full use* of gaming values—strength, intelligence, wisdom/luck, constitution, dexterity, charisma, and hit points— and multiple pathways for each option for the most complete experience in gaming books, as fully realized heroes quest through the most famous worlds of fantasy!

**With an introduction by
Isaac Asimov**

ENTER THE ADVENTURE!

TOR'S CROSSROADS™ ADVENTURE SERIES

ROBERT HEINLEIN'S
GLORY ROAD
FATE'S TRICK

by
Matt Costello

A TOM DOHERTY ASSOCIATES BOOK
NEW YORK

FATE'S TRICK

Crossroads Game/novels are published by Tor Books by arrangement with Bill Fawcett.

A TOR Book
Published by Tom Doherty Associates, Inc.
49 West 24 Street
New York, NY 10010

Cover art by David Cherry

ISBN: 0-812-56452-9   Can. ISBN: 0-812-56453-7

Library of Congress Catalog Card Number: 88-50991

First edition: December 1988

Printed in the United States of America

0 9 8 7 6 5 4 3 2 1

PARALLEL UNIVERSES

In a way, human beings have always conceived of parallel universes. Any place that can't be reached from *our* place and where the laws of nature may be different from our own is a parallel universe. Legends of a "fairyland," or a "spirit world," or an "underworld" where the shades of the dead gather, are, in a way, tales of parallel universes.

Or we might think of Heaven as a place of eternal bliss where the spirits of the blessed will join the angels and be with God—and is that not a parallel universe? Might not the same be said of Hell?

John Milton, in his great epic, *Paradise Lost*, pictures Heaven, Hell, and Earth as three spheres, three parallel universes, separated by Chaos, and even pictures Satan as travelling through Chaos when he goes from Hell to Earth—with all the feel of an interplanetary voyage.

But what does science have to say? Can there be parallel universes in reality? Suppose we do a little speculating. . . .

The one universe we know is our own, and that is supposed to have started about fifteen billion years ago as a tiny point of matter that exploded in a Big Bang giving us a universe made up of a hundred

v

billion or so galaxies that are still hurrying apart, impelled by the remaining force of that long-ago blast.

Where did that original point of matter, containing all the mass and energy that now fills our vast universe, come from? The latest suggestion is that it arose as a quantum fluctuation out of nothing. If that were so we might imagine a "super-universe" consisting of nothingness—a truly infinite quantity of nothingness.

Somewhere in that nothingness there is a quantum fluctuation and in an unimaginably small fraction of a second it expands and becomes our universe which is still expanding today and is now billions of light-years from end to end. It may be that our universe will not expand forever, but that its expansion will steadily slow under the pull of its own gravity, so that finally, eons from now, the expansion will come to a halt. The universe will then very slowly begin to contract, and do so faster and faster until, in additional eons, it will come together in a "Big Crunch" and pass out of existence—fading back into the infinite nothingness from which it came.

But if there can be one quantum fluctuation in nothingness, surely there can be another—and another . . . In fact, we can imagine that in infinite nothingness there are infinite fluctuations and the formation of an infinite number of universes.

The infinite nothingness can be viewed as a panorama of boiling, with bubbles appearing here and there, each one expanding, then contracting and disappearing. Different bubbles may be of different size, of different mass, and endure for lifetimes of different extents. Each bubble may have its own laws of nature, randomly different from those in others. Each bubble may be permanently self-enclosed and separate so that there can be no communication across the nothingness that separates them. And our own universe is one of these evanescent bubbles.

And what if, somehow, communication between universes is established? What an opportunity for a science fiction writer to imagine a universe operating under different laws of nature. In fact, I once tried this myself in my novel *The Gods Themselves* (Doubleday, 1972).

Yet mighty as this picture of an infinite number of parallel universes is, there is another way of imagining parallels that is even stranger and, in my opinion, more mind-boggling.

Probably every one of us has speculated on the "ifs" of life. What if I hadn't decided to attend a certain meeting. I might never have met the young woman who eventually became my wife. What if, at reaching a certain corner, I had stooped to tie my shoelace and missed noticing a certain event which, in actual fact, I *had* noticed and which had changed my life. What if your father had not been turned down by a certain girl and married your mother on the rebound—so that you had never been born.

There are an infinite number of possibilities in your personal life.

Or what if a particular battle had gone just a little differently, a general had made a different decision, a small group of men had done this rather than that, so that the South had won the Battle of Gettysburg, or the British army had been captured at Dunkirk, or the Athenians had been smashed at Marathon? What if the Chinese had landed in California long before Columbus had landed in the Bahamas? What if the Romans had invented the steam engine?

There are an infinite number of possibilities in history generally, and each possibility might be viewed as initiating a parallel universe—one in which the Chinese dominate, or the Roman Empire resulted in a permanently unified Europe, or the United States existed as a group of constantly quarreling fragments, and so on.

Actually, such things may not be entirely a matter of imagination. In quantum theory, there is now believed to be a certain "weirdness." There is no way of telling exactly how an electron may react, and it is possible that no decision is reached as to its particular action until it is observed. It may be that every event involving every subatomic particle in the world may move unpredictably in one of at least two and perhaps very many directions and that each one of those alternate events may start our universe in a slightly different direction. In other words, each one of trillions of trillions of events every second may represent a branch point of our universe and there may be an incredibly large number of possible or potential universes, following different paths at every one of these branch points and all equally real in some mind-boggling way. We occupy *one* universe out of all the potential universes that may exist.

I once based a science fiction novel on that concept, too. It was *The End of Eternity* (Doubleday, 1955).

You now have in your hands a parallel-universe tale, entitled *Fate's Trick,* in which you have alternate procedures that you may choose after the fashion of modern quantum weirdness. Enjoy!

—Isaac Asimov

INTRODUCTION AND RULES TO CROSSROADS™ ADVENTURES

by Bill Fawcett

FOR THE MANY of us who have enjoyed the stories upon which this adventure is based, it may seem a bit strange to find an introduction this long at the start of a book. What you are holding is both a game and an adventure. Have you ever read a book and then told yourself you would have been able to think more clearly or seen a way out of the hero's dilemma? In a Crossroads™ adventure you have the opportunity to do just that. *You* make the key decisions. By means of a few easily followed steps you are able to see the results of your choices.

A Crossroads™ adventure is as much fun to read as it is to play. It is more than just a

1

game or a book. It is a chance to enjoy once more a familiar and treasured story. The excitement of adventuring in a beloved universe is neatly blended into a story which stands well on its own merit, a story in which you will encounter many familiar characters and places and discover more than a few new ones as well. Each adventure is a thrilling tale, with the extra suspense and satisfaction of knowing that you will succeed or fail by your own endeavors.

THE ADVENTURE

Throughout the story you will have the opportunity to make decisions. Each of these decisions will affect whether the hero succeeds in the quest, or even survives. In some cases you will actually be fighting battles; other times you will use your knowledge and instincts to choose the best path to follow. In many cases there will be clues in the story or illustrations.

A Crossroads™ adventure is divided into sections. The length of a section may be a few lines or many pages. The section numbers are shown at the top of a page to make it easier for you to follow. Each section ends when you must make a decision, or fight. The next section you turn to will show the results of your decision. At least one six-sided die and a pencil are needed to "play" this book.

The words "six-sided dice" are often abbreviated as "D6." If more than one is needed a number will precede the term. "Roll three six-sided dice" will be written as "Roll 3 D6." Virtually all the die rolls in these rules do involve rolling three six-sided dice (or rolling one six-sided die three times) and totaling what is rolled.

If you are an experienced role-play gamer, you may also wish to convert the values given in this novel to those you can use with any fantasy role-playing game you are now playing with. All of the adventures have been constructed so that they also can be easily adapted in this manner. The values for the hero may transfer directly. While fantasy games are much more complicated, doing this will allow you to be the Game Master for other players. Important values for the hero's opponents will be given to aid you in this conversion and to give those playing by the Crossroads™ rules a better idea of what they are facing.

THE HERO

Seven values are used to describe the hero in gaming terms. These are strength, intelligence, wisdom/luck, constitution, dexterity, charisma, and hit points. These values measure all of a character's abilities. At the end of these rules is a record sheet. On it are given all of the values for the hero of this adventure and any equipment or supplies they begin the adventure with. While you adventure, this record can be used to keep track of damage received and any new equipment or magical items acquired. You may find it advisable to make a photocopy of that page. Permission to do so, for your own use only, is given by the publisher of this game/novel. You may wish to consult this record sheet as we discuss what each of the values represents.

STRENGTH

This is the measure of how physically powerful your hero is. It compares the hero to others in how much the character can lift, how hard he can punch, and just how brawny he is. The strongest a normal human can be is to have a strength value of 18. The weakest a child would have is a 3. Here is a table giving comparable strengths:

Strength	Example
3	A 5-year-old child
6	An elderly man
8	Out of shape and over 40
10	An average 20-year-old man
13	In good shape and works out

15	A top athlete or football running back
17	Changes auto tires without a jack
18	Arm wrestles Arnold Schwarzenegger and wins

A Tolkien-style troll, being magical, might have a strength of 19 or 20. A full-grown elephant has a strength of 23. A fifty-foot dragon would have a strength of 30.

INTELLIGENCE

Being intelligent is not just a measure of native brain power. It is also an indication of the ability to use that intelligence. The value for intelligence also measures how aware the character is, and so how likely they are to notice a subtle clue. Intelligence can be used to measure how resistant a mind is to hypnosis or mental attack. A really sharp baboon would have an intelligence of 3. Most humans (we all know exceptions) begin at about 5. The highest value possible is an 18. Here is a table of relative intelligence:

Intelligence	Example
3	My dog
5	Lassie

6	Curly (the third Stooge)
8	Somewhat slow
10	Average person
13	College professor/good quarterback
15	Indiana Jones/Carl Sagan
17	Doc Savage/Mr. Spock
18	Leonardo dá Vinci (Isaac Asimov?)

Brainiac of comic-book fame would have a value of 21.

WISDOM/LUCK

Wisdom is the ability to make correct judgments, often with less than complete facts. Wisdom is knowing what to do and when to do it. Attacking, when running will earn you a spear in the back, is the best part of wisdom. Being in the right place at the right time can be called luck or wisdom. Not being discovered when hiding can be luck; if it is because you knew enough to not hide in the poison oak, wisdom is also a factor. Activities which are based more on instinct, the intuitive leap, than analysis are decided by wisdom.

In many ways both wisdom and luck are further connected, especially as wisdom also measures how friendly the ruling powers of the universe (not the author, the fates)

are to the hero. A hero may be favored by
fate or luck because he is reverent or for
no discernable reason at all. This will
give them a high wisdom value. Everyone
knows those "lucky" individuals who can
fall in the mud and find a gold coin. Here
is a table measuring relative wisdom/
luck:

Wisdom	Example
Under 3	Cursed or totally unthinking
5	Never plans, just reacts
7	Some cunning, "street smarts"
9	Average thinking person
11	Skillful planner, good gambler
13	Successful businessman/Lee Iacocca
15	Captain Kirk (wisdom)/Conan (luck)
17	Sherlock Holmes (wisdom)/Luke Skywalker (luck)
18	Lazarus Long

CONSTITUTION

The more you can endure, the higher your
constitution. If you have a high constitution you are better able to survive physi-
cal damage, emotional stress, and poisons.
The higher your value for constitution,
the longer you are able to continue func-

tioning in a difficult situation. A character with a high constitution can run farther (though not necessarily faster) or hang by one hand longer than the average person. A high constitution means you also have more stamina, and recover more quickly from injuries. A comparison of values for constitution:

Constitution	Example
3	A terminal invalid
6	A 10-year-old child
8	Your stereotyped "98-pound weakling"
10	Average person
14	Olympic athlete/Sam Spade
16	Marathon runner/Rocky
18	Rasputin/Batman

A whale would have a constitution of 20. Superman's must be about 50.

DEXTERITY

The value for dexterity measures not only how fast a character can move, but how well-coordinated those movements are. A surgeon, a pianist, and a juggler all need a high value for dexterity. If you have a high value for dexterity you can react quickly (though not necessarily correctly), duck well, and perform sleight-of-hand magic (if you are bright enough to learn how). Conversely, a low dexterity means you react slowly and drop things frequently. All other things being equal, the character with the highest dexterity will have the advantage of the first attack in a combat. Here are some comparative examples of dexterity:

Dexterity	Example
3 or less	Complete klutz
5	Inspector Clouseau
6	Can walk and chew gum, most of the time
8	Barney Fife
10	Average person
13	Good fencer/Walter Payton
15	Brain surgeon/Houdini
16	Flying Karamazov Brothers
17	Movie ninja/Cyrano de Bergerac
18	Bruce Lee

Batman, Robin, Daredevil and The Shadow all have a dexterity of 19. At a dexterity of 20 you don't even see the man move before he has taken your wallet and underwear and has left the room (the Waco Kid).

CHARISMA

Charisma is more than just good looks,

though they certainly don't hurt. It is a measure of how persuasive a hero is and how willing others are to do what he wants. You can have average looks yet be very persuasive, and have a high charisma. If your value for charisma is high, you are better able to talk yourself out of trouble or obtain information from a stranger. If your charisma is low, you may be ignored or even mocked, even when you are right. A high charisma value is vital to entertainers of any sort, and leaders. A different type of charisma is just as important to spies. In the final measure a high value for charisma means people will react to you in the way you desire. Here are some comparative values for charisma:

Charisma	Example
3	Hunchback of Notre Dame
5	An ugly used-car salesman
7	Richard Nixon today
10	Average person
12	Team coach
14	Magnum, P.I.
16	Henry Kissinger/Jim DiGriz
18	Dr. Who/Prof. Harold Hill (Centauri)

HIT POINTS

Hit points represent the total amount of

damage a hero can take before he is killed or knocked out. You can receive damage from being wounded in a battle, through starvation, or even through a mental attack. Hit points measure more than just how many times the hero can be battered over the head before he is knocked out. They also represent the ability to keep striving toward a goal. A poorly paid mercenary may have only a few hit points, even though he is a hulking brute of a man, because the first time he receives even a slight wound he will withdraw from the fight. A blacksmith's apprentice who won't accept defeat will have a higher number of hit points.

A character's hit points can be lost through a wound to a specific part of the body or through general damage to the body itself. This general damage can be caused by a poison, a bad fall, or even exhaustion and starvation. Pushing your body too far beyond its limits may result in a successful action at the price of the loss of a few hit points. All these losses are treated in the same manner.

Hit points lost are subtracted from the total on the hero's record sheet. When a hero has lost all of his hit points, then that character has failed. When this happens you will be told to which section to turn. Here you will often find a description of the failure and its consequences for the hero.

The hit points for the opponents the hero meets in combat are given in the adventure.

You should keep track of these hit points on a piece of scrap paper. When a monster or opponent has lost all of their hit points, they have lost the fight. If a character is fighting more than one opponent, then you should keep track of each of their hit points. Each will continue to fight until it has 0 hit points. When everyone on one side of the battle has no hit points left, the combat is over.

Even the best played character can lose all of his hit points when you roll too many bad dice during a combat. If the hero loses all of his hit points, the adventure may have ended in failure. You will be told so in the next section you are instructed to turn to. In this case you can turn back to the first section and begin again. This time you will have the advantage of having learned some of the hazards the hero will face.

TAKING CHANCES

There will be occasions where you will have to decide whether the hero should attempt to perform some action which involves risk. This might be to climb a steep cliff, jump a pit, or juggle three daggers. There will be other cases where it might benefit the hero to notice something subtle or remember an ancient ballad perfectly. In all of these cases you will be asked to roll three six-sided dice (3 D6) and compare the total of all three dice to the hero's value for the appropriate ability.

For example, if the hero is attempting to juggle three balls, then for him to do so successfully you would have to roll a total equal to or less than the hero's value for dexterity. If your total was less than this dexterity value, then you would be directed to a section describing how the balls looked as they were skillfully juggled. If you rolled a higher value than that for dexterity, then you would be told to read a section which describes the embarrassment of dropping the balls, and being laughed at by the audience.

Where the decision is a judgment call, such as whether to take the left or right staircase, it is left entirely to you. Somewhere in the adventure or in the original novels there will be some piece of information which would indicate that the left staircase leads to a trap and the right to your goal. No die roll will be needed for a judgment decision.

In all cases you will be guided at the end of each section as to exactly what you need do. If you have any questions you should refer back to these rules.

MAGICAL ITEMS AND SPECIAL EQUIPMENT

There are many unusual items which appear in the pages of this adventure. When it is possible for them to be taken by the hero, you will be given the option of doing so. One or more of these items may be necessary to the successful completion of the adventure. You will be given the option of taking these at the end of a section. If you choose to pick up an item and succeed in getting it, you should list that item on the hero's record sheet. There is no guarantee that deciding to take an item means you will actually obtain it. If someone owns it already they are quite likely to resent your efforts to take it. In some cases things may not even be all they appear to be or the item may be trapped or cursed. Having it may prove a detriment rather than a benefit.

All magical items give the hero a bonus (or penalty) on certain die rolls. You will be told when this applies, and often given the option of whether or not to use the item. You will be instructed at the end of the section on how many points to add to or subtract from your die roll. If you choose to use an item which can function only once, such as a magic potion or hand grenade, then you will also be instructed to remove the item from your record sheet. Certain items, such as a magic sword, can be used many times. In this case you will be told when you obtain the item when you can apply the bonus. The bonus for a magic sword could be added every time a character is in hand-to-hand combat.

Other special items may allow a character

to fly, walk through fire, summon magical warriors, or many other things. How and when they affect play will again be told to you in the paragraphs at the end of the sections where you have the choice of using them.

Those things which restore lost hit points are a special case. You may choose to use these at any time during the adventure. If you have a magical healing potion which returns 1 D6 of lost hit points, you may add these points when you think it is best to. This can even be during a combat in the place of a round of attack. No matter how many healing items you use, a character can never have more hit points than he begins the adventure with.

There is a limit to the number of special items any character may carry. In any Crossroads™ adventure the limit is four items. If you already have four special items listed on your record sheet, then one of these must be discarded in order to take the new item. Any time you erase an item off the record sheet, whether because it was used or because you wish to add a new item, whatever is erased is permanently lost. It can never be "found" again, even if you return to the same location later in the adventure.

Except for items which restore hit points, the hero can only use an item in combat or when given the option to do so. The opportunity will be listed in the instructions.

In the case of an item which can be used in every combat, the bonus can be added or subtracted as the description of the item indicates. A +2 sword would add two points to any total rolled in combat. This bonus would be used each and every time the hero attacks. Only one attack bonus can be used at a time. Just because a hero has both a +1 and a +2 sword doesn't mean he knows how to fight with both at once. Only the better bonus would apply.

If a total of 12 is needed to hit an attacking monster and the hero has a +2 sword, then you will only need to roll a total of 10 on the three dice to successfully strike the creature.

You could also find an item, perhaps enchanted armor, which could be worn in all combat and would have the effect of subtracting its bonus from the total of any opponent's attack on its wearer. (Bad guys can wear magic armor, too.) If a monster normally would need a 13 to hit a character who has obtained a set of +2 armor, then the monster would now need a total of 15 to score a hit. An enchanted shield would operate in the same way, but could never be used when the character was using a weapon which needed both hands, such as a pike, longbow, or two-handed sword.

COMBAT

There will be many situations where the hero will be forced, or you may choose, to meet an opponent in combat. The opponents can vary from a wild beast, to a human thief, or an unearthly monster. In all cases the same steps are followed.

The hero will attack first in most combats unless you are told otherwise. This may happen when there is an ambush, other special situations, or because the opponent simply has a much higher dexterity.

At the beginning of a combat section you will be given the name or type of opponent involved. For each combat five values are given. The first of these is the total on three six-sided dice needed for the attacker to hit the hero. Next to this value is the value the hero needs to hit these opponents. After these two values is listed the hit points of the opponent. If there is more than one opponent, each one will have the same number. (See the Hit Points section included earlier if you are unclear as to what these do.) Under the value needed to be hit by the opponent is the hit points of damage that it will do to the hero when it attacks successfully. Finally, under the total needed for the hero to successfully hit an opponent is the damage he will do with the different weapons he might have. Unlike a check for completing a daring action (where you wish to roll under a value), in a combat you have to roll the value given or higher on three six-sided dice to successfully hit an opponent.

For example:

Here is how a combat between the hero armed with a sword and three brigands armed only with daggers is written:

BRIGANDS
To hit the hero: 14 To be hit: 12 Hit points: 4

Damage with   Damage with
daggers: 1 D6   sword: 2 D6
(used by the brigands) (used by the hero)
There are three brigands. If two are killed (taken to 0 hit points) the third will flee in panic.

If the hero wins, turn to section 85.

If he is defeated, turn to section 67.

RUNNING AWAY

Running rather than fighting, while often desirable, is not always possible. The option to run away is available only when listed in the choices. Even when this option is given, there is no guarantee the hero can get away safely.

THE COMBAT SEQUENCE

Any combat is divided into alternating rounds. In most cases the hero will attack first. Next, surviving opponents will have the chance to fight back. When both have attacked, one round will have been completed. A combat can have any number of rounds and continues until the hero or his opponents are defeated. Each round is the equivalent of six seconds. During this time all the parties in the combat may actually take more than one swing at each other.

The steps in resolving a combat in which the hero attacks first are as follows:

1. Roll three six-sided dice. Total the numbers showing on all three and add any bonuses from weapons or special circumstances. If this total is the same or greater than the second value given, "to hit the opponent," then the hero has successfully attacked.

2. If the hero attacks successfully, the next step is to determine how many hit points of damage he did to the opponent. The die roll for this will be given below the "to hit opponent" information.

3. Subtract any hit points of damage done from the opponent's total.

4. If any of the enemy have one or more hit points left, then the remaining opponent or opponents now can attack. Roll three six-sided dice for each attacker. Add up each of these sets of three dice. If the total is the same as, or greater than the value listed after "to hit the hero" in the section describing the combat, the attack was successful.

5. For each hit, roll the number of dice listed for damage. Subtract the total from the number of hit points the hero has at that time. Enter the new, lower total on the hero's record sheet.

If both the hero and one or more opponents have hit points left, the combat continues. Start again at step one. The battle ends only when the hero is killed, all the opponents are killed, or all of one side has run away. A hero cannot, except through a healing potion or spells or when specifically told to during the adventure, regain lost hit points. A number of small wounds from several opponents will kill a character as thoroughly as one titanic, unsuccessful combat with a hill giant.

DAMAGE

The combat continues, following the sequence given above, until either the hero or his opponents have no hit points. In the case of multiple opponents, subtract hit points from one opponent until the total reaches 0 or less. Extra hit points of damage done on the round when each opponent is defeated are lost. They do not carry over to the next enemy in the group. To win the combat, you must eliminate all of an opponent's hit points.

The damage done by a weapon will vary depending on who is using it. A club in the hands of a child will do far less damage than the same club wielded by a hill giant. The maximum damage is given as a number of six-sided dice. In some cases the maximum will be less than a whole die. This is abbreviated by a minus sign followed by a number. For example D6−2, meaning one roll of a six-sided die, minus two. The total damage can never be less than zero, meaning no damage done. 2 D6−1 means that you should roll two six-sided dice and then subtract one from the total of them both.

A combat may, because of the opponent involved, have one or more special circumstances. It may be that the enemy will surrender or flee when its hit point total falls below a certain level, or even that reinforcements will arrive to help the bad guys after so many rounds. You will be told of these special situations in the lines directly under the combat values.

Now you may turn to section 1.

RECORD SHEET

Alex Tanen

Strength: 13
Intelligence: 15
Wisdom: 12
Constitution: 11
Dexterity: 15 (16 for sleight of hand)
Charisma: 11

Hit Points: 16

Items Carried: Materials for five prestidigitation tricks:
1. Changing Kerchief
2. Multiplying Rabbits
3. Cards
4. Disappearing Wand
5. String Cutting

This may be the worst booking I have ever had. Yes, performing magic at the Osceola Florida Senior Citizens Center has to be right down near the bottom of the gig barrel.

I mean, here I am keeping up a steady patter, trying to run through my abbreviated, budget-level magic routine (no "beautiful" assistant in spangled tights, no big mechanical tricks involving trunks, trapdoors, and disappearing elephants). But when I see the retirees chatting to each other, comparing tans and floral shirts, I know it's going to be a tough afternoon.

Then, when I ask for a volunteer from the audience to come up for some up-close card magic, I get this yokel who announces to his friends, "I see how he does it, Harry. He's got these funny cards, a rigged deck. Hah, you can't fool me."

No, sir, I think—my smile firmly in place—no way I can make a monkey out of a horse's—

And then the people start getting up, actually standing up and walking to the back, to what is supposed to be a postshow buffet. Before long, it's a regular dinner theater, and my show has the sound effects of snapping celery and popping dentures.

Somehow I get through the act and stumble off the ministage to the deafening roar of indifference.

As I said, this is about as close to the bottom of my professional career as I hope to ever see. After picking up my princely check ($150, if you must know), I leave Osceola hoping never again to see that particular tropical garden spot.

Now, despite this gig, I'm not such a bad magician. In fact, in conjuring circles I'm considered something of an innovator. I've introduced a few striking variations in classic acts (including a saw-the-woman-in-three trick that wowed them at the Golden Nugget) and I've uncovered a few secrets that old Harry Houdini never meant to be revealed.

But my stage personality, at least according to my agent, my manager, and my former mother-in-law, leaves something to be desired. I'm too cocky, perhaps, not so much interested in charming an audience with "showmanship" as in tricking them. Magicians tend to have a modest air about them, a winning smile that says, "Sure it's a trick, and you could easily figure it out . . . why sure, if only you got off your big fat behind and pored over my equipment."

While I, on the other hand, tend to radiate a smug superiority. My tricks are my art, and when I perform I'll stun, shock, and surprise an audience. But humility just isn't my strong suit.

After that afternoon show, I make my way back to the Breakwater Motel, which looks like the kind of place Norman Bates might set up if he moved to sunny Florida. There's free cable (but no HBO), one of those generic soft mattresses that plays havoc with my back, and a small bathroom "sanitized" regularly every A.M. whether I want it or not. It's a serviceable abode for the next few days before I head back to New York.

When I open my door, I see that there's a letter, addressed to Alex Tanen c/o the Breakwater Motel. Amazing, I think, since absolutely no one knows where I'm staying. (I'm at a fiscal stage in my life where I try to control just who knows where I am.)

But the letter is clearly addressed to me. And what's more incredible, it looks like one of those massive sweepstakes mailings, with dollar signs all over the place proclaiming that I may be eligible to possibly win thousands of dollars. Only, I see as I open it, I'm wrong. It's a million dollars, and I have already won.

According to this strange letter, personalized no doubt by some highly efficient computer, I, Alex Tanen of the Breakwater Motel, have won the grand prize in the Universal Publishers Sweepstakes, a prize of at least one million U.S. dollars.

Then I read it again, and sure enough it says I've already won the prize. No, "might be a winner" or "eligible to win." I've won it, plain and simple. All I have to do is call the toll-free number printed at the bottom of the letter and collect my loot.

Section 1

I check this ever-more improbable letter for an address. There's a Miami P.O. box but that's all. Needless to say, I quickly decide to invest a quarter to see how bright my future might be.

I stroll over to the pay phone inside the motel office, aware that, unfortunately, the desk clerk will hear at least half the conversation. (Already, like Scrooge McDuck, I'm plotting to keep my riches secret.) But she barely looks up from her *Enquirer* as I walk over to the phone. A small color set next to her is displaying the ongoing tragedies of some L.A.-type studs and strumpets.

I plop the quarter in and dial the 800 number.

It rings twice, and then someone answers. The voice is thin, tentative, not at all the cheery, bumptious sound of your typical phone salesperson.

"Hello," I say. "I just received notification that I won—"

"Mr. Tanen?" she asks.

"Why, yes. I was calling to claim—"

"Yes, your prize. We've been expecting you to call. We're all ready for you. But time is important. We'd like to meet you tonight, to arrange the award."

This sounds good to me. "Sure. I have a show tonight on the *Hollywood Princess*. But for a million bucks I'd gladly cancel."

"No. We'll come to your performance. We'd *like* to see you perform. Then, we can arrange everything else."

I wonder for a moment, cautiously ('cause I'm a big city boy, thank you, with no interest in being flimflammed), just what "everything else" might be. But the woman moves right along.

"We'll see you tonight and meet you after your show."

"Wait! What's your name?"

She seems to pause, and a bit of hesitation comes back into her voice. "Palina."

"Great, Palina. I'll look forward . . ."

But she's gone, and for some reason I don't feel like I should begin counting my newfound wealth.

Roll 3 D6.

If the total is equal to or less than Alex's value for Intelligence, turn to section 9.

If the total is greater than his value for Intelligence, turn to section 17.

* **2** *

I turn almost too quickly, and find myself
face-to-face with something that I really imagined lived only in nightmares after an evening
of too much food and drink.

It looks human. Sort of. I mean, it has a
nose, eyes, and ears (I think). But the skin is a
deep dull grey, and the eyes are a fiery orange,
like the electric bulbs in the eye sockets of a
fun house clown.

But my quick look costs me. I get to see the
intruder, but I don't see the nasty club he
brings down on my head.

Turn to section 13.

* **3** *

Nice crowd, I think, watching them scoop up forkfuls of lettuce with the house's "special dressing," something bought in bulk from the nice folks at Winn Dixie. But it's very much a typical tourist group. A smattering of young families, with kids less interested in the great voyage than shooting little wheels of cucumber at unsuspecting diners at adjacent tables. And older couples, enjoying the freedom having grown children brings, spending money and trying to act frivolous.

But no mysterious (perhaps beautiful) woman sitting alone, a nice check for one million dollars in her purse.

Once again, I remind myself that things don't happen this way. It has to be a hoax, or some kind of gimmick or trick.

I make my way to the claustrophobic back-stage area (also used by the busboys who like to sneak a smoke).

"Mr. Tanen," a voice booms out. It's Louis —no last name, just Louis—the manager of this floating extravaganza. "I trust that you are ready for the big show?"

"Yes, sir. Just stretching my legs a bit."

He edges closer to me, his cologne a veritable stench in the narrow passageway. "I'd like us to start a bit early tonight. There may be a storm. We may have to shorten the trip by a half hour or so." He grins, displaying a mouthful of overly white teeth. I know what he's worried about. The old *Hollywood Princess* is a riverboat, and the bay, though generally placid, can kick up nastily in a tropical storm. Outside of the passengers, the *Princess* carries little weight, almost nothing below the waterline. It makes the paddle wheeler move economically, but in choppy water it can be a pretty sick ride.

"No problem, Lou. Five minutes okay? I'll just check a few things and then you can introduce me."

After another semi-dazzling smile, Louis turns.

I go to my small dressing closet (there's no way you can call it a room). Everything looks set for the performance, everything that is except the small box I keep my dove in.

It's upside down. I right it and wonder how it might have been turned over. Then I open the lid gingerly and check the small bird.

It's dead.

And for the second time today, I feel that my life is taking a few unexpected turns.

Turn to section 18.

* 4 *

I think, oddly enough, of a suave, debonair Cary Grant. Just what did he do in *North by Northwest* when he was trapped in a car, heading downhill on U.S. 1 with no brakes. And he also had the double disadvantage of being completely soused.

Unfortunately, I can't remember, although I seem to recall his driving right into a row of hedges and having a tough time explaining to the police just what had happened.

If I live I'll have an even tougher time explaining this.

I grab the steering wheel, feeling perfectly foolish. There's no way through the steady stream of trucks and cars. A glance to my right confirms the sickening fact that a big bus is indeed heading my way.

First I swerve left, just narrowly missing the bus, but my rear end smashes against a Mercedes 230SL. I laugh out loud, giddy and amazed at my survival so far.

Then one of those caravan wagons that families have acquired as the latest suburban necessity heads right toward my door.

I had tried the brakes—totally whacked out

of fear (and it's true, time does slow down when you are about to die). But not the accelerator. I squash it; the car lurches ahead ever so slightly, and the happy caravan family misses me by what must have been mere millimeters.

Then it's open-road time again, and the car's increased speed makes it even more impossible to control.

Just ahead I see what might be my only chance. It's some kind of pond, with a few cows grazing stupidly nearby. (I don't mean to malign the poor animals, but in my accelerated condition their lazy cud chewing seems intolerable.)

It might be wet and muddy enough, I reason, to stop my car without sending my skull through the windshield.

It's that, or cannonballing down the road until a better idea leaps to mind.

If Alex tries to stop the car in the pond, turn to section 16.

If not, turn to section 8.

* **5** *

Those lips, those eyes . . . if love be the fruit of life play on . . . I think, not caring about mixed metaphors or dangerous alluring femme fatales in hot cars.

"Sure," I say.

I slide into the car, tossing my magic stuff in the backseat with the kid who Palina introduces as her sister Tam. I shut the door.

Palina pulls away like a rocket, pasting my wet body against the seat. "Slow down," I offer. "We're not in any rush." There's nothing light in her face now. It's tight, grim, and I begin to have second thoughts about my recent decision-making.

"That's what you think," she corrects me.

Turn to section 11.

* **6** *

"Did you see who did it?"

"Unfortunately, I did." I wonder whether my beautiful booking agent here might not find what I was about to say a bit farfetched.

"He, or maybe I should say it, had something definitely wrong with its skin—it was all grey and bumpy. It reminded me of one of the mollusks from that movie *The Time Machine.*"

Palina looks back at Tam and shrugs.

"You know, the green guys. Anyway, the horror movie reject also had a foul smell about him. Is he a friend of yours?"

Palina laughs (a sound worth waiting for).

"Hardly. Just be glad you got away from him."

"Real glad," Tam agrees.

"So now, tell me why I'm here."

"Because," Palina says, looking right at me, "we need you."

Add +2 to the next Wisdom roll Alex makes and turn to section 31.

* **7** *

Sleight of hand doesn't always mean sleight of foot, and I catch enough of a look at the nasty clublike thing above my head to know that it will take some fancy movement to avoid being brained by it.

I push myself against the wall (it isn't that far away) while the club slashes the shadows. I watch it crash into the box with my dove, and a horrible chirp signals the end of my assistant's career in magic.

Whoever it is stands in the shadows, and all I can see are two eyes that look, I swear, to be bright orange. Then he, she, or whatever it is disappears, dashing away. After a moment's pause (where I consider the various pluses and minuses to giving pursuit), I dash out into the hall, bumping right into Louis.

"Mr. Tanen, everything is, I trust, all ready. We have a small problem . . ."

"Did you see someone—" I start to say, then I catch myself. I may want to play this barge again. While I know I did nothing to provoke such a nasty attack, who knows whether Louis, with his oily slick hair and badly capped teeth, might think I'd been in trouble with the law, or some loan shark, or even with what club owners euphemistically refer to as "the organization." I quickly decide to keep my mouth shut.

"See what?" Louis asks, his eyebrows expressing mild alarm.

"Oh, nothing," I say casually. "I just asked one of the kids for a soda. Sea air makes my larynx a bit tight."

He looks at me strangely, then continues. "What I wanted to ask you, Mr. Tanen, was to get your show on a bit early. The weather's looking bad, and we may have to bring our wonderful patrons back to shore early. And we do want them to have the whole experience of the *Hollywood Princess*."

Excluding tossing their cookies overboard during a tropical squall, I think.

"No problem. I'll just need a few minutes to double-check everything, and then we can go on with the show."

"Great, Mr. Tanen. I'm sure the audience will love you."

Louis turns, and I know that all through my act I'll have two people to look for. Palina, if indeed she shows up, and my friend with, so help me, orange eyes.

Turn to section 18.

* **8** *

It's a nice stretch of road, no lights, no cars, no moms crossing with baby carriages. The rain has stopped, and it seems almost okay to be barreling down the highway at ninety-five plus miles per hour. Almost, except for the railway tracks just ahead with the great lumbering freight train crawling along.

I'll be there in a minute.

I roll down the window, inhale deeply, and, raising a hand to wave out the window, I yell—

"Good-bye!"

Turn to section 29.

* **9** *

I hang up the phone, bothered by more than one thing. I've been around enough to know that such wildly fortuitous things just don't happen. Luck can be a factor in determining fame and fortune, but just didn't happen that way.

Then there was Palina's accent. Very odd indeed, like someone from France trying to sound like a Westport, Connecticut Yuppie. Odd, and inviting. Her voice was decidedly different, intriguing, and, who knows, perhaps even dangerous.

But my prospects are such that, outside of a general air of caution, I can proceed to the evening performance and my million-dollar rendezvous knowing that nothing better is in the offing.

Turn to section 19.

* **10** *

The backstage area resembles the sumptuous quarters of the washrooms on the Staten Island Ferry. There's just about enough space for my equipment, including my portable magic table, and a small box to hold my dove. The secret to an effective magic routine is no surprises. It would be more than a little embarrassing to reach into one's pocket for an egg, or a bouquet, or the ace of spades, and find only a few subway tokens and a stub for the Loew's 86th Street theater. So, I check and recheck, until it borders on becoming compulsive activity.

Only now, as I mentally check off all my gear, I notice that someone has touched it. Almost imperceptibly, everything has been moved.

Perhaps a busboy, I wonder, or Louis, stage manager of this floating extravaganza.

But then, I feel, in that awful way that you sometimes do, that someone is right behind me.

Naturally, I try to turn around.

Roll 3 D6.

If the total is equal to or less than Alex's value for Dexterity, but above 6, turn to section 7.

If the total is six or less, turn to section 2.

If the total is greater than his value for Dexterity, turn to section 13.

* **11** *

I sit in the car, patiently, waiting for either Palina or the kid in the back to say something. After what seems like more than a polite pause, I speak.

"Let me guess," I say. "There's no million-dollar prize."

Palina seems to be having difficulty handling the car, as if it were something novel. I'm about to suggest that perhaps she might like to go slower.

"No contest," she agrees, "but there is a million dollars. Tam, give Alex the money."

"Here you go," the girl says, letting a pile of hundred-dollar bills plop onto my lap. She giggles, and then snaps her gum next to my right ear.

"That's ten thousand," Palina says.

"Not quite, Palina. I bought some gum on the dock," Tam explains.

Palina gives her a withering stare. "My sister sometimes forgets what we're here for."

"That's good," I smile good-naturedly, "because I haven't the foggiest idea why I'm here. And why you're throwing money in my lap. And why someone killed my bird."

She looks at me. I want to scream for her to please return her eyes to the road.

"So they *do* know. That explains everything. You're in great danger. The bird was just a warning. There's not much we can do to protect you here." A leg, slim and powerful, pushes down the accelerator.

"There are speed limits," I suggest. "South Florida police don't look too kindly on maniacs behind the wheel."

"We're late."

For a very important date, I surmise.

"Like for what? If you don't mind my asking."

"Tell him, sister, he's got to know sooner or later." Tam pops a pink bubble and then licks the filmy wreckage off her face.

"Okay, Alex. You'll be paid one million dollars for a very special magic performance, very far from here."

"Very far," Tam giggles.

"When you're done, we'll bring you back."

"And the bird?"

"A warning. There are people who would prefer you didn't come with us."

"Yeah, and I might be one of them."

If Alex didn't see anything of who tampered with his magic equipment, turn to section 12.

If he saw just the eyes, turn to section 15.

If he saw the whole face, turn to section 6.

* **12** *

"Did you get a look at who did it?"

"No, I'm afraid I arrived too late for that. But look, you haven't explained why I'm so important. There are dozens of stage magicians who'd make monkeys appear in your underwear for a million bucks."

Tam laughs, and rolls back into her seat.

Palina looks right at me, her eyes glowing and her voice gentle, promising. "But we want *you.*"

Turn to section 31.

* **13** *

There's no room to maneuver, and the club, or something very much like a club, is coming straight down on my head.

I've only been knocked out once before in my life. It was in Vietnam, but not in combat. Combat and I stayed strangers. I was in a little bar called The Hot Spot, which, besides offering sloe-eyed maidens pressed into servicing American soldiers, also featured a walk down a secluded alleyway where someone waited with a metal pipe wrapped in cloth. It was cushioned because the club owners didn't want any real trouble with the authorities. But it was heavy enough to give you twelve hours of real solid shut-eye, and a monster of a headache in the A.M.

Sans money, wallet, and maybe even shoes, I woke up from my evening at The Hot Spot in an alleyway, joining the legion of history's sadder and wiser soldiers. Within weeks, I'd be laughing at the new arrivals' horror stories of being waylaid in the darkened corners of Saigon. Live and learn.

This clubbing is less vehement, but no less effective. I can feel a buckling in my knees.

Section 13

The next thing I know I'm being roughly shaken awake.

"Mr. Tanen, please wake up. You've been drinking, no? You can't do this to the *Princess.* We have a reputation—"

I blink a few times to reduce the number of Louises (that's the stage manager who was shaking me) from three to two, and finally to a slightly fuzzy one.

"Jeez, my head," I groan. I let pudgy Louis try to pull me up. I'm about to tell him of my incident when I freeze. Trouble, even if you didn't bring it on yourself, is an unwelcome commodity at a club. It's easier to get rid of the act than to determine who did what to whom.

"Just catnapping," I smile at Louis.

He looks unconvinced. "We need to start the show early, in just a few minutes. The weather," he says, licking his lips, "is supposed to turn bad. A big storm is coming."

I know what he's worried about. The *Princess,* which carries no ballast to speak of, is a sick sight when the bay turns rough.

I resist an urge to rub the growing knob on the back of my cranium. "I understand, Louis. Show time in five minutes. No problem."

He forces a smile and strolls away. I turn around to check my gear. Everything appears in order. Everything, except the small box holding my dove.

It's upside down. I right it, feeling the dull thud of something rolling around inside. I open the lid slowly, and feel inside.

The bird is dead. The end of its magic career and, I think, the beginning of God knows what for me.

Turn to section 18.

* **14** *

It was much too tricky a maneuver. There's a nifty Mercedes 230SL coup moving as fast as possible down Lauderdale Avenue, and a bus neatly slicing in the other direction.

I'm in the middle.

The Mercedes pushes my car's rear end slightly to the right, while the bus chugs on, and over, my now out-of-control heap.

At the moment, I have only one thought.

The bus driver must think I'm some kind of maniac.

Turn to section 29.

* **15** *

"Did you see who did it?"

"Sort of. I mean I noticed the club, and then, in the shadows, I could make out the weirdest eyes—all orange and glowing."

"And that's all?"

"That's it. Oh, there was a strange smell in the hallway, but that could have been leftovers from the galley. So now tell me, why am I here?"

"Because," Palina says, looking right at me, "we want you."

Add +1 to the next Wisdom roll Alex makes. Turn to section 31.

∗ **16** ∗

As anyone who's ever jumped off the Brooklyn Bridge could have told me, water can be a pretty hard substance.

The murky pond, with cows in attendance, does indeed, stop the car. My head, though, continues moving into the steering wheel and then beyond, just narrowly avoiding the windshield.

But I'm alive. At least, I think I am.

When I come to, I'm sitting in the passenger seat next to Palina.

"We pulled you out of your car," she says softly.

"And cleaned you up," the kid says, holding up a bloody bit of cloth.

Palina gestures at the young girl. "My sister, Tam. She was quite worried about you, even though she knew you would be fine."

"Oh, she did, did she. I'm glad she can foretell the future."

"Yes," Palina casually concurs. "So am I."

Turn to section 11.

* **17** *

Hanging up the phone, I feel a familiar, and dangerous, longing. Not for money, though I'm getting a little worried that my glory days as a performer are behind me.

Women, on the other hand, have quite often been my downfall. I seem to have a knack of falling totally out-of-control in love with soulful creatures who end up turning me inside out. Instead of hooking up with some bouncy, level-headed Girl Scout turned career woman, I seek out the neurotic, doomed "artist" to re-enact *Tristan and Isolde* in modern dress while we drink $30 bottles of Chateauneuf de Pape.

And this lady sounds like she might just be my type.

And that's bad news.

Turn to section 19.

* **18** *

"Ladies and gentlemen, Mr. Randolph Kovaks and Associates, owners of the *Hollywood Princess,* are pleased to present, for your entertainment pleasure, Alex Tanen's World of Magic!"

Louis's voice sounds even tinnier coming through the boat's cheap P.A. system than in person. Of course, the diners continue to eat even as I make my appearance on stage. As many times as I've performed in a dinner theater setup (and let's face it, that's the way Mom and Dad in America like their theater— with a thick slab of prime rib), I can never get used to the sound of food being gummed to death in lieu of applause.

"Thank you, thank you . . . you're too kind," I say to what I imagine are a few enthusiastic claps. The single spotlight is pointed right at my face, making it nearly impossible to see the crowd (usually a good thing), but even as I run through my routine, I try to see if there is someone out there who is following my act with unusual attention.

Despite my lack of concentration, the show moves along nicely. I make a bouquet of flowers appear in some tubby fellow's back pocket, and a nice, neat-as-a-pin little boy is a perfect foil for my multiplying rabbit trick. His face lights up like a light bulb when I tap his closed fist and he opens it to find five foam-rubber rabbits.

But the "silk into liquid" effect brings everyone, including the bustling waiters, to a stop. It's my most expensive effect, but when the silk cloth is poured out of a cup of liquid, it's a knockout. The applause after that is solid.

I come back for an encore (as prescribed in my contract with Mr. Ralph Kovaks and Associates) and decide to do a little magic involving psychological forces.

The procedure, known to every stage magician, is simple. Present the illusion of choosing a number to someone in the audience, even as you trick them into selecting exactly the number you want.

I ask for a volunteer from the audience.

"I will." It's that voice, that odd accent, clear and unmistakable, coming from the back of the dining room, my million-dollar lady. I even think that the audience has grown quiet. "Yes," I say, taken aback. "Step closer please . . . near the front." She comes, and though I can't hear that well, I know enough to know that I'm a goner. If she has any interest in controlling my soul, it's hers to play bocci with.

Her hair is a deep, lustrous black, and her bright blue eyes glow catlike just outside the pool of light made by the spot. I barely notice a small kid, a scruffy-looking girl standing next to her.

"In this trick," I announce, struggling to regain my performance momentum, "I will guess a number you have on your mind. Are you ready?"

Her eyes lock onto mine and she whispers, "Yes," as if it were the answer to a more profound question than the one I asked.

"Think of any number between one and fifty. It must be a two-digit number, with both digits odd and they must not be alike. You cannot, for instance, pick eleven."

Now, the odds are the unsuspecting audience member will say thirty-seven. By mentioning eleven, you psychologically "force" the person to jump up to the next group of possible digits. Once there, thirty-seven is the number most commonly chosen, followed by thirty-five.

And I have both numbers in my rear pockets, one in the left, one in the right, ready to stupefy the audience when she makes her selection. Then I see her smile, not a malicious grin, but a coy, playful thing.

"Fifteen," she says.

"Fifteen," I respond dully. Well, there goes my big finish. But even as I look at her, I see something more in her eyes, some sign of encouragement. "And what, if I may ask, is your age?"

Her grin broadens. "Twenty-two."

"Twenty-two and fifteen adds up to—" I

announce with a great flourish. I turn to a cigar-chomping patron squatting near me. "Sir, would you reach into my left pocket."

He looks around sheepishly before reaching in my pocket and pulling out an oversize card with the number thirty-seven on it.

"Thirty-seven," I announce. And the audience applauds.

I look up to see the woman, but she's gone. Even as I bow, I try to see through the smoky haze.

"Mr. Alex Tanen, ladies and gentlemen. How about a really big hand for—"

I make my way backstage.

By the time I have my gear packed up (and the poor bird discarded with the table scraps), the *Hollywood Princess* is bobbing in the water like a toy boat. It has turned around early, but the storm is moving at a faster pace than the leisurely paddle wheeler. Patrons are giving each other bizarre looks, recognizing that the fun might be over and the hatches, if there are any, had better be battened down.

After I collect my evening's pay from Louis (a substantial $325, minus a $22 union fee), the acrid aroma of Chicken Kiev *redivivus* wafts through the night air, mixing with the crisp smell of rain and ozone.

Soon the small choppy waves in the bay are breaking over the side of the boat, and each new lurch causes the crowd to groan outloud.

"I guess you lost this bunch as repeat customers," I laugh to Louis.

The band finishes the song, "You Are the Sunshine of My Life"—and seems to fumble around without starting another. "They've got to begin playing," Louis hisses, bustling over to the band leader.

It's getting like the *Titanic,* except if it comes to lifeboats, I'm going to take my chances swimming to shore. Hell, it's only a couple of hundred yards or so away. Only now, the old *Hollywood Princess* isn't tooting its horn, and the dockside barbecuers are cozily inside, behind their sliding glass doors, seeing what Vanna is wearing tonight.

The mystery lady, to my chagrin, is nowhere in sight. I even ask Louis if he's seen her, but he's too preoccupied with his ongoing nautical tragedy to even hear what I'm asking.

Fortunately, the dock appears in the mist (with some of the lurching patrons actually shouting, "There it is! We're here. We've made it.") The captain, to his credit, does an estimable job of docking the flat-bottom behemoth, taking his time to position the boat close enough to be lashed, but not so close that it will be heaved against the dock.

The gangplank is barely in place before the hoards of happy sailors literally slosh off the *Princess.* Louis abandons his familiar post at the exit. These people are in no mood to hear the words, "Come back and see us again."

Not having eaten, I'm having an easier time of it, but I hurry off to try and catch sight of my mystery lady. But as the parking lot empties,

Section 18

I'm left with the bizarre feeling of having imagined both her and whoever tampered with my bird.

I'm about to walk over to my rent-a-wreck when I hear a car screaming toward me.

It's one of those Japanese Z-cars, a kind of everyman's sports car. Plenty of power under the hood, but minus the classic lines of a Corvette or a Jaguar. It barrels up to me much too fast on the wet pavement and screeches to a halt.

The passenger door pops open, and the driver leans over.

"Mr. Tanen . . . I believe we had an appointment?"

It's the woman from the magic act. She is perfectly dry, and the kid (what's with the kid? I wonder) is in the backseat looking on with interest.

"You are Palina?"

She nods. "If you'll get in, I'll explain everything."

I can see her more closely now, her long dark hair, blue eyes, and what I suspect is an absolutely outrageous body hiding under her businesslike skirt and blouse.

But I have enough sense to pause a moment. What, after all, do I know about her? By now, I suspect that the million-dollar prize is some kind of "come-on." If that's the case, what are they up to?

So, for a moment, I stand in the rain, getting soaked through, staring at Palina, feeling more than a bit undecided.

Roll 3 D6.

If the total is equal to or less than Alex's value for Wisdom, turn to section 5.

If the total is greater than his value for Wisdom, turn to section 20.

* **19** *

The *Hollywood Princess* is, so I'm told, a real-live paddle wheeler. But instead of tooting up and down the Mississippi, it navigates Ft. Lauderdale Bay, gently passing the sun-bleached homes of pleasure-boat owners (who seem to never tire of coming out and waving at the tourists—or maybe they're paid to come out—befrocked in a barbecue apron, spatula in hand, as the *Hollywood Princess* steams by).

Besides a dinner of Chicken Kiev and baby peas, the *Princess* also offers what is billed as "Vegas-style" entertainment. Most nights, that consists of some Borscht Belt refugee making an endless string of wife jokes, alternating with an act offering, for your listening pleasure, the song stylizations of a group with the improbable name of The Three Deuces. But tonight, probably to save the sanity of the beachboys cum waiters, was to be something different. I, Alex Tanen, magician extraordinaire, am booked to make rabbits vanish along with the dinner rolls and carrot sticks.

I select some specialty items for the show, knowing that my mysterious benefactor will be watching. First, there's my liquid silk scarf trick, an expensive bit of trompe l'oeil that never fails to impress the leisure-suit set. And the magic dove routine, with a special twist featuring a real dove that appears in the air (and I hope I don't lose this bird to the balmy Florida sea air—they're expensive).

I arrive at the dock just a few minutes before sailing.

The night turns out to be unseasonably cool, not the sunset voyage the patrons were hoping for. After stowing my gear, I go and stand by the ship's oaken bar downing endless club sodas while the paddle wheeler's crew (all decked out in cute white and blue outfits that remind me of James Mason's crew in *20,000 Leagues Under the Sea*) make ready to leave.

Just as soon as the *Princess* leaves the dock, the waiters begin serving meals, accompanied by the raucous hooting of the vessel's whistle.

Naturally, I scour the crowd for some sign of the mysterious (and, I trust, beautiful) Palina.

If Alex walks around the dining area, turn to section 3.

If Alex checks the backstage area, turn to section 10.

* **20** *

Too weird, I think. The dark-haired beauty, the kid, the dead bird.

"Look, why don't I call you later and we can talk some more. All I want to do now is get home, shower, get some dry clothes, and get a new bird."

I back away from Palina's car, but I can see that she doesn't look too happy. The kid is leaning forward, saying something to her. "Yeah, I'll just give you a buzz later."

"Mr. Tanen . . . Alex . . . you must come with us . . ." she calls.

I back away and walk over to my heap. I jump in and turn the key, groaning when the engine refuses to catch. "C'mon, baby," I whisper, a bit scared now. Even my normally bad judgment tells me that this lady could be bad news.

The car stumbles to life like a drunken bum being kicked awake ("Okay, okay, I'm moving, ossifer, just tell me where up is"). I want to get away from the mystery lady and back to the wonderful world of Florida shopping malls.

Then something really interesting happens. My car won't stop. The first time I go through a red light, I think it has to be due to my own preoccupation with getting away. But then I fly past an intersection (eyes closed, mind you) narrowly avoiding two cars and a Tastee Freeze truck.

And yes, turning the ignition key off does nada, and the brake is totally ineffectual. Steering, though, seems to be functional, and so, except at intersections, which are simply too awful to watch, I try to keep my automatic bullet on a "straight" path.

When I come to the intersection of Lauderdale Avenue and Route 22, I know that the end is near. (It's a dream, I pray, nothing more than one of those crazy, cockamamy dreams. Sure, I'll just open my eyes and it will all be over.) But a steady stream of very realistic traffic is moving east and west on Lauderdale. What I have to do is slip right through without hitting anyone.

For this intersection, I know I have to keep my eyes open.

Roll 3 D6.

If the total is equal to or less than Alex's value for Dexterity, turn to section 4.

If the total is greater than his value for Dexterity, turn to section 14.

* **21** *

If you never spent time standing in murky swamp water at night, surrounded by alligators (and wondering, all the time—do they eat people?), well, it's one of those life experiences best left unsavored.

I'm all for getting out of the swamps as quickly as possible, only there's no way to do that without facing the alligator. The fact that I have a cutlass in my hand does little to encourage me. But Palina senses my concern and provides just the right motivational jolt.

"If you don't want to finish your life in the belly of an alligator, I suggest you start using your cutlass."

As if to drive the point home, the energetic alligator nearest me opens its maw, displaying an impressive array of teeth.

Needless to say, I'm ready to play jungle boy.

The only thing I wonder is where you hit an alligator to stop it—and not just make it angrier.

The alligator nearest Alex is about to attack.
To hit Alex: 8   To be hit: 10   Hit points: 8

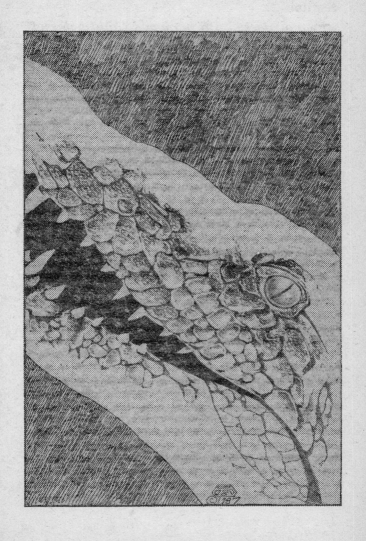

Section 21

Alligator does: 1 D6 damage   Cutlass does 1 D6 damage

Alex's cutlass, unknown to him, is +1 to hit since it has been personalized for his use. The alligator is hungry but not that hungry. It will leave after losing half its hit points. Alex gets the first attack and combat is not simultaneous.

If Alex is wounded, turn to section 36.

If Alex's hit points are reduced to 0, turn to section 29.

If Alex wounds the alligator, turn to section 22.

Continue combat until one of the above happens.

* **22** *

It's amazing what fear can do. The cutlass feels light and natural in my hand, as if I were experienced at swordplay and derring-do.

What's more, I feel a ruddy glow of satisfaction when I see the blade puncture the creature just below its mouth—when it turns its throat to me. I'm all for preserving our natural resources. I'd never buy a pair of alligator shoes, and I don't even use a handbag. But all the gloves come off when nature starts encroaching on my space, thank you.

If the alligator has lost half its hit points, turn to section 37.

If not, return to section 21 for another round of combat.

* **23** *

I take a breath. It's more than disconcerting to go from fighting alligators in a dismal, dank swamp to facing some horned nasty that's a new entry in my catalog of zoological monstrosities.

"Go for the soft spot . . . in its forehead!" Palina shouts.

I turn to her, still not completely tuned into the situation. She and Tam seem to have dispatched a few of the horned beasts already. Mine looks bigger, and meaner, but that could simply be my up-close perspective.

Good thing my cutlass is already out. Now if I can just hit the creature's so-called soft spot, everything will be great.

Turn to section 32.

Alex is + 1 to hit in the upcoming battle, and he attacks first.

* **24** *

If there's a time to play my trump card, I figure this is it.

"Sorry, guys, but until I get some answers, I'm afraid I'll have to bow out. Catch you later, after your swim." I pull the cutlass out of its sheath and drop it onto the walkway.

Then I briskly walk back to the car.

To my great disappointment, I don't hear the sound of Palina and Tam struggling out of the muck and chasing after me. Still, I feel better walking back to the car, the highway, and away from Pogo's Playground.

As fate would have it, I don't quite make it back.

I hear a scream. At least, it sounds like screaming, two voices ringing through the humid air.

Amazingly enough, I reach for the short cutlass—which isn't there. I'm no Boy Scout, but I know when duty calls.

I run back to the opening, and try to find my cutlass. For a moment, it looks like it is gone, perhaps carried off by some raccoon interested in self-defense. But then I see it, half on, half off the wooden walkway.

Section 24

I pick it up, and with nary a thought, I jump into the swamp. The first sensation is one of sinking into muck, like stepping onto rubber cement that sucks and grabs at my feet. But then, prompted by the screams, I start moving through the slime.

I see them and, for a moment, can't see what all the fuss is about. Both Palina and Tam have their swords held out in front of them.

"What's the problem?"

"That," Palina says flatly.

"That" is a good-sized alligator, and its teeth glisten nicely in the water. It snaps at Palina, who jabs at its mouth.

"There're more coming," she says, gesturing to her left. "And this one's blocking the way."

"And you want me to get rid of it?" I say, disbelieving.

"No. You take Tam past while I keep it occupied. Then I'll follow."

"Why don't I just bring her back to the walkway?" I argue. But I turn around to notice two pairs of eyes sliding through the water right at me.

What a great night this is turning out to be, I think.

Turn to section 21.

* **25** *

I try to dodge the juggernaut coming toward me, while getting ready for another blow.

Roll 3 D6.

If the total is equal to or less than Alex's value for Dexterity but greater than 5, turn to section 27.

If the total is below 6, turn to section 38.

If the total is greater than his value for Dexterity, roll for damage.

If Alex is still alive (has hit points left), return to section 32 for another round of combat.

If Alex's hit points are reduced to 0, turn to section 29.

* **26** *

Maybe it's time to get some answers before I proceed any further in this junket.

Besides, jumping in the water doesn't seem to be a particularly healthy course of action.

Maybe there's another way to the island.

Turn to section 30.

* **27** *

I dodge, not as well as Escamillo might have, but I neatly avoid that Horned Ghost's left horn.

Its right horn, though, cleanly catches me in my side, and the ghost quickly removes it, ready to dive in again.

Alex has just been gored for 1 D6 hit points of damage.

If he is still alive, return to section 32 for another round of combat.

If he has been killed (his hit points are down to 0), turn to section 29.

* **28** *

Roll 3 D6.

If the total is less than or equal to Alex's value for Dexterity, turn to section 33.

If the total is greater than Alex's value for Dexterity, and the Horned Ghost is still alive, return to section 32 for another round of combat.

If the Horned Ghost has been slain, turn to section 40.

* **29** *

We all have different ideas of death.

Me, I always imagined, or hoped, that the Grim Reaper would come gently in the night, while I was well into my severe dotage, and take me just as a show was ending in my dream theater. In other words, I didn't want to know about it.

But it was not fated to be. I had become a reluctant hero.

The worst part of a hero's death is the pain. The best part is you're not bored at the moment of your passing.

You may return to the beginning of Fate's Trick *to start the adventure again. Perhaps this time fate will be kinder to Alex.*

* **30** *

"Come, Alex. It's time."

It's amazing what placing a beautiful woman in a swamp will do for her natural allure.

All of a sudden, I don't feel so compelled to join them.

"Come *on*, Alex. I don't like standing here," Tam urges.

I put my hand on my cutlass.

Alex must decide if he is going to follow them into the water or if he is going to backtrack to the car, perhaps getting some answers to what it's all about.

If Alex decides to follow them, turn to section 39.

If Alex decides to walk away, turn to section 24.

* **31** *

I think everyone's had that uncomfortable feeling where they begin to think they're being sold a bill of goods. Maybe it doesn't come all at once. No, it's just a gradual, unsettling feeling that you are being made a total ass of.

Surely that's how I feel now, driving through the slowly changing Florida night, due south. Miami is far behind us, and I can't believe where Palina says she is taking me.

(And all the time I feel like saying: Let's drop the kid off at a video arcade and pick out some sleazy motel with magic fingers in the bed and a mirror on the ceiling.)

But Palina quietly informs me that we are going to the Everglades. The swamp. Complete with alligators, water snakes, and all sorts of creepy crawlies. And what makes it even more marvelous is that we're going at night.

Can my life get any more wonderful?

Of course, all my questions (and I do have a few points to raise in regards to the evening's adventure) have to be deferred. I'll be told everything later, she assures me. But Tam's giggles from the back seat do anything but alleviate my anxiety.

Section 31

So, do I ask to be let out . . . to get off this Magical Mystery Tour?

No. For three reasons. First, I have $10,000 sitting on my lap, with the promise of approximately $990,000 more if I go along. Second, whoever doesn't want me to go might be taking steps to see that I don't get any second thoughts. It might be difficult to inform them that I'm no longer part of the deal. And last, (and in my callow heart I know most important) I don't think I can bear getting out of the car and never seeing Palina again. My brain is filled with fevered visions of the two of us getting really friendly later on, perhaps when my show is over. Once, as she is trying to reassure me, she reaches over and touches my knee and I damn near feel sparks.

So I stay in the car, ask a few questions (most of which are politely ignored), and watch my mystery lady tear up the highway leading to the Everglades National Park.

The inside car light is on, and Tam has a map spread out.

"It's here, Pal. The next parking area should be real close."

I look back and forth, first at Palina, then at Tam. The next parking area is going to be all right for what? For digging up bodies from the swamp? For an air shipment of cocaine from our nice friends in Colombia?

(And where is the park ranger? Shouldn't he be swooping down on us?)

We're halfway into the park, along the two-lane highway that leads from the park entrance to Flamingo, a gulf-side tourist town, with a visitors' center, restaurant, and souvenir shops.

All we have seen driving in are the spooky, glowing eyes of barred owls perched alongside the road. The night has cleared completely, and in a few hours it will yield to a spectacular dawn.

If I'm here to see it.

"There!" Tam shouts. "Park there."

"Why here?" I ask, knowing that, from past experience, it is unlikely that my question will be answered.

"Because this is where . . . we're being met."

Yeah, by whom? I think. Dracula? The Swamp Thing?

"And what about the forces of evil that want to stop me?" I laugh.

She doesn't. She stops the car altogether and quickly kills the light. "They may be here already. If you see someone, just remember that it's a construct. By the laws of the Twenty Universes, it can't kill you, not directly. But it can make things dangerous for you."

"And they're so ugly," Tam says, popping open the door. Despite my general nonaffinity for the younger set, I'm developing a begrudging admiration for Tam. She must be ten or eleven, and obviously a very sharp cookie. Her brown hair, much finer than her sister's, is cropped close. She also has a nice knack for editorializing on her sister's more serious announcements. Gallows humor in the young is such an endearing quality.

But the fact that she seems to know a lot more about what is going on than I'm being told is mighty annoying.

"The constructs can't do anything to kill you directly," Tam says. "It's just impossible for them, here at any rate."

"Pardon my ignorance, but would you mind telling me what a construct is?"

The sisters look at each other like conspirators. Palina nods, and Tam, a pint-sized born lecturer, explains.

"They're like golems, almost machines really. But they have enough biological stuff so they live, kind of. Mediocre reasoning ability, and not much facility with geometric abstractions—"

"That's for sure," Palina agrees.

"But they're pretty ugly in a fight. Fortunately"—Tam pops a bubble—"they can't do anything too much to us. Not directly at least."

I'm wondering what "not directly" means when Palina grabs my magic gear and stuffs it into what looks like a purple and yellow backpack. Then, rather abruptly, she starts walking into the swamp.

"What's she—" I start to ask Tam (who is beginning to seem more and more like the voice of reason), but she is trooping after her sister.

"C'mon, Alex, we don't have a lot of time."

For what, I want to ask. But knowing the question will be ignored, I follow along.

Now, the Everglades is one of the places on the planet that is incredibly spooky in the middle of the sunniest day. It can be blue sky overhead, with big, puffy, friendly clouds. But in the swamp, walking its trails, well, it's like being lost on some strange planet where humans aren't due on the evolutionary cycle for another 50 million years.

And the fact that there are alligators plopped in the muck about you doesn't help that image at all.

The trails of the Everglades are, in most cases, only narrow wooden boardwalks that let visitors stroll through the mangroves and all over the murky puddles. A high protective railing and wire mesh keeps you and the alligators separate, but it still isn't Disney World.

"Strange place for a magic show," I mumble.

"What's that?" Palina yells back.

I repeat my comment. "Who's the lucky audience, wolverines and wombats?"

"There are no wombats here," Tam explains.

"Oh, that's nice. Maybe I can get one of the cormorants to stand in for my dead dove."

Palina has stopped, right over a narrow rivulet. Without a moon, I can't see much of the water. Of course, I imagine that every glistening spot is a 'gator. For all I know, they could be.

"That's it," Palina says, turning to me. She points to what appears to be a small island about a hundred yards away.

"What's that?" I ask.

"Where we have to go."

Tam digs around in her backpack and pulls out some wire clippers. She starts, rather proficiently I think, to cut the mesh.

"What are you doing?" I ask, turning to her.

"I can't place wards, so we'll just have to move as quickly as possible," Palina says. "But you better take this just in case."

This is the evening's most absurd twist so far. Palina reaches in the backpack and pulls out a small curved sword, not much bigger than a large Bowie knife. It comes with a sheath and a leather strap, all of which look new.

"How thoughtful," I say. "And it's not even my birthday."

Both she and Tam are strapping on similar swords. "You'd prefer something longer, a rapier perhaps?"

"Oh, no, no, please don't trouble yourself. This is just fine. Just what the doctor ordered."

"Good," she smiles, apparently missing my sarcasm.

Then Palina and Tam crawl through the open mesh and drop into the water.

"Let's go, Alex."

Right. Sure. I'm going to jump into the Everglades with all my wilderness pals.

Roll 3 D6.

If the total is less than or equal to Alex's value for Wisdom, turn to section 34.

If the total is greater than his value for Wisdom, turn to section 26.

* **32** *

There are eight or ten of the beasts (Horned Ghosts, I later learn they are called). But we have our backs to a cliff, and only a few can get their licks in at a time.

Still, I wonder how we'll be able to fight them one after the other, until they are all gone. The first Horned Ghost has picked itself off the ground and is looking me over. Horned Ghosts are omnivorous, and even though they have armlike appendages, they rely on their horns to do most of the damage for them. As Tam and Palina claim their first kill, some of the others, to the rear, rip it apart while those closest to us press forward. My personal Horned Ghost brings his head down, and arcing its great broad back, it starts to charge forward.

I nervously finger the hilt of my blade. I have just one shot to get it before I become a human shish kebab.

I raise my sword high over my head, scream (for who knows what reason), and strike.

HORNED GHOST
To hit Alex: 7   To be hit: 9   Hit points: 12

Damage with horns: 2 D6 − 2   Damage with cutlass: 1 D6

Alex attacks first, followed by the Horned Ghost. Combat is not simultaneous.

If Alex hits, turn to section 28.

If the Horned Ghost strikes, turn to section 25.

Continue combat until one or the other hits.

* **33** *

I never knew I was such a skilled sportsman. (Or is it, as they say, not the mechanic but the tool?) At any rate, my sword feels like part of me, and I bring it home neatly, plunging right into the Horned Ghost's soft spot.

It stops dead in its tracks, staggers backward, and then finally collapses into the dust.

The other Horned Ghost pulls it backward (and apart), and there is the revolting sound of snapping sinews and breaking bones.

Another ghost moves into position, and I ready my sword again.

But an oddly familiar voice rings out over the snorting din.

Turn to section 40.

* **34** *

A few thoughts run through my head, none of them particularly logical.

Something strange is going on here. Something dangerous. To me. Okay, it would be nice if they told me what was happening. But failing that, it might be wisest to trust Palina and her sister. Besides, who knows what's really waiting for me back at the car?

Turn to section 30.

* 35 *

My knees buckle. I don't want them to, but this is getting a bit too much for someone whose most recent greatest thrill has been hitting a New York Instant Lotto for ten bucks.

The horned creature seems almost to be grinning—or maybe that's simply the natural sneer of its snout—and is preparing to gore me.

Palina grabs my arm and yanks me away.

The horn spears the red, dusty soil and Palina barks in my ear, "Get up, Alex! Get up and use your weapon! Tam can't hold them back forever."

I look at Tam, flashing her blade back and forth like some wine-crazed buccaneer. She has to be the most amazing ten-year-old I've ever seen. The sight inspires me to get off my bottom.

"Go for the soft spot, on the forehead," Palina says.

My legs hold, the cutlass feels sure in my grip, and I'm ready to face the horned animals.

Turn to section 32.

* **36** *

I don't feel it at first.

No, the soft, squishy sound of the alligator's teeth suddenly puncturing my thighs and pressing down is like something happening far away . . . over there to someone else.

But the wild, excited look in its eyes (I mean, this baby is close to me) and the gooey stuff pouring out of my leg tells me that another chomp and I can forget about being ambulatory for a while.

I bring my cutlass up for another jab at the alligator.

Return to section 21 for another round of combat.

* **37** *

The alligator seems like it's withdrawing, a sullen, brooding creature. Then it slides away. Either it's dead, or it decided it could be just as happy eating spotted frogs, all things considered.

I turn around quickly, Errol Flynn of the marsh, ready to help Palina and Tam. But they're both standing there, broad grins on their faces.

"Where are the other alligators?" I ask, ready to save them from danger.

"We chased them away," Tam announces proudly. "They didn't like it when we bopped them on the nose with our swords."

"C'mon, Alex, we've already lost too much time. We'll have to hurry if we're to make it."

Make what I want to ask, but I know that, for the nonce, questions are verboten.

I follow Palina as she takes great long strides, pulling her feet out of the muck and stepping toward the small, scruffy island ahead. Tam walks beside me, less stuck down due to her light weight.

"Pal thinks the alligator might have been sent," Tam says quietly. "But I don't think so.

I couldn't sense anything else there, nothing but hunger."

"Yeah. I felt their hunger too. But I thought they, whoever they are, couldn't directly hurt me."

"Alex, using an alligator is *not* directly hurting you."

"Well, excuse me . . ."

Palina reaches the island and grabs a snaky vine to haul herself out. Tam has a bit of difficulty clambering out, and I push her up until she can crawl onto the semisolid surface of the island.

"Careful," Palina says. "There's a small pool there to your left. Might be quicksand."

I follow Tam onto land, feeling ever so grateful to be out of the water. I wish I had brought along a change of pants. (But then, I didn't expect to be going on a holiday.)

Palina is using a stick to draw symbols in the dirt. It looks like half of a baseball diamond, with the pitcher's mound and first and second base. Tam inscribes some strange runes inside it that resemble hieroglyphics.

"Okay, I'll bite. What are you two crazy kids doing now?"

"It's time," Tam says.

"Right. Alex, stand there," Palina orders, gesturing at first base. "Tam, take your place. Have your swords ready."

"Oh, of course. How could I be so stupid to forget," I say, once again unsheathing my short cutlass. "Now can you tell me what's up?"

"We're going someplace, Alex. Not on

Section 37

Earth. Not even in this galaxy. It will take just a minute. And then," she smiles, "you will have some answers."

"Right. Whatever you say, my swamp princess. Do we have to fly there?"

"No," Tam answers, very serious now. "But, Alex, try not to move at all. It will feel better."

"Well, I'm sure—"

I stop. It's a bit like the feeling you get when you've been sitting down for a long time and you get up much too quickly. Just like that, only about ten times more powerful. I bring my hands up to my head just to make sure it's still there, attached to my shoulders.

"What is this?" I ask, but I can't hear my own voice. I start to vocalize, trying to see why no sounds come out of my mouth. "Ah . . . Ee . . . Oo . . ." I think I'm saying, but I hear nothing.

Then the feeling ends.

And I'm looking right into the face of a Texas longhorn standing on two clumpy feet. In the two seconds I have for careful observation (before looking around and screaming for Palina), it looks like a minotaur out of the Wild West. It stares at me too, eyes glistening in the bright sunlight, nostrils flaring, before it pulls back, ready to gore me on its twin horns.

Roll 3 D6.
If the total is less than or equal to Alex's value for Constitution, turn to section 23.
If the total is greater than his value for Constitution, turn to section 35.

* **38** *

I back up, flush against the cliff face, ready to face the worst from the charging Horned Ghost. But fate rewards me with a fortuitous thought.

If I turn sideways, the Horned Ghost's twin horns might go completely around me and plunge harmlessly into the cliff. It's my only chance, so I take it. I raise my arms over my head and I turn sideways just at the moment the tips of the horns are about to reach me. And my body squeezes—just barely between them. Now, unfortunately, the Horned Ghost's foul breath is inches away from me. But despite its eagerly snapping jaws, it can't reach my flesh. Its clumsy almost-hands try to hold on to me.

I bring my sword down once again just as the Horned Ghost turns to back away from the cliff.

Return to section 32 for another round of battle.

Alex's Dexterity will be at +1 for the next attack only.

* **39** *

"Okay, I'll come, but let me go on record as saying that this is a bad idea."

I jump down into the muck, which seems to suck eagerly at my shoes. To move is like walking through fudge. But Palina and Tam keep up a surprisingly brisk pace. The island is close, inviting despite its dismalness.

We're about ten yards away when the first alligator snaps at Palina. She jerks her arm out of the way just in time. Luckily she noticed the swish of its tail in the water. The second time it surfaces, she has her cutlass ready. I'm confused enough to just stand there watching them until Tam kicks me.

"Get your sword up . . . there's more coming!"

And sure enough, right behind me, I see two pairs of jellylike eyes gently gliding in my direction.

Turn to section 21.

* **40** *

"Deftly done—for a beginner."

I know that voice, I'm sure of it. I look through the mass of Horned Ghosts (also turned in the direction of the sound), but all I can see is someone dressed in what looks like an odd mixture of Davy Crockett's buckskin and Robin Hood's green tights.

The Horned Ghosts are soon flying left and right, some just stumbling over each other to get away—and can tell that this guy is bad news—while others are receiving properly administered blows to the forehead. In what seems a second, what remained of the herd is scattered or dead.

"Well, Alex, I'm sorry you had such an unpleasant arrival, but welcome to the Nevia Valley."

"Dad," Tam yells, dropping her bloody sword on the ground and running over to the man.

"Tam, my Tam . . . you were supposed to stay back, behind your sister."

"I know, but I thought he," she says, pointing in my direction, "might need my help."

"And well he might," the man says, grinning, returning to look at me.

I take some steps toward him. About my height, sandy blond hair, broad shoulders, and powerful arms that carry a heavy double-edged sword as long as his daughter.

I know this man. But I'll be damned if I can remember from where.

"Oscar," Palina says, going over to him and kissing his cheek. They seem the same age. Are they husband and wife? But no, Tam called him Dad, and Tam is Palina's sister. And I'm sure that I know no Oscar.

But then I remember.

"Easy Gordon," I whisper. His grin broadens, pleased that I remembered. "I thought you were dead," I say.

"Not dead, Alex, and while you travel around here you best call me Oscar, Consort to the Empress of the Twenty Universes."

He extends his hand.

I met Evelyn Cyril Gordon when he was about to be cashiered out of the army. It was in the early days of the "police action" in Vietnam, before all hell broke loose. I had just arrived, and plopped into the easy job of writing gung ho profiles for *Stars & Stripes*. Gordon (whose initials E.C. had turned into a rakish "Easy") had performed admirably in a midnight skirmish with some NVA irregulars.

(Later he told me he was just trying to get his grunts to a shady, dry spot upriver. Go figure.)

Needless to say, he had no interest in trifling with me. He told me to make up whatever I wanted and be done with it.

Which is exactly what I did. Then, surprisingly, he asked me to hit the bars with him, where we sampled, under his expert tutelage, all the sensations of the fleshpots of Saigon.

(And, no, I didn't get rolled that night. That came during my second visit.)

Easy told me his view of the soon-to-be war, which was ahead of the time by about five years.

The next time I saw Gordon it was a week or two later, while he was still awaiting orders to go stateside. He came to a magic show my commanding officer had persuaded me to stage.

We were almost friends, and when he ended up in the Riviera, I even got a postcard or two from him. Before he disappeared, that is, and even his parents had given him up for lost.

Now he's here, nearly twenty years later. And despite the Horned Ghosts, and this odd world, there's really only one thing that bothers me. No, make that two things.

First, why in the world is he called Oscar? And second, how come he doesn't look a day over twenty-two?

"My wife Star named me," he laughs good-naturedly, taking quick strides through the woods. The woods we are walking through, by the way, seems more or less normal, except for these tiny purple mushrooms that dot the forest floor. I see Tam scoop one up now and then and pop it into her mouth. "She noticed my scar, and either she or I said, 'Oh, scar.' The rest is history."

"You say she's an empress?" I ask.

"Oh, yes. The locals call her 'Her Wisdom.' She's got the experience and knowledge, good and bad, of 7,000 years of emperors and empresses."

"She must be a fun person to have an argument with."

He laughs again, and I find myself amazed at his youth. That is surely my next question.

"She leaves her work at the office. But sometimes, when she's absorbed in one of the old emperor's vitae from the cube, it can leave her a bit schizoid for a week or so. But she needs all that background if she's going to rule intelligently over the Twenty Universes."

I reach down, following Tam's example, and start to put one of the purple mushrooms into my mouth. Oscar reaches over and casually swipes it away.

"Tam was born here. Her stomach can handle them. It would give you a powerful stomachache and the runs like you never had before."

"Thanks," I say, remembering another bad trip, to Acapulco. "Just what are the Twenty Universes, and how'd you get here?"

Our party—consisting of Palina and Tam in the front, Oscar, myself, and a few burly fellows bringing up the rear—has started climbing the hill.

"Not long now, Alex, and you can change your clothes, get some food, and"—a small smile creases his face—"tend to any of your other needs. To answer your question, and excuse me if I'm brief but I'll tell you all later: there are twenty known universes, and our earth is merely one of them. Some are quite like ours, like here, in the Nevia Valley. Others resemble versions of hell. They are all accessible by means of gates—passageways, if you will—that open for a few minutes, ranging from every few weeks to every few years. You came here via the one in the Everglades. You'll be leaving here by way of one on the other side of that mountain—" He points into the distance, where snowcapped mountains brood on the horizon. "I was brought here, recruited really, as a . . . mercenary," he laughs. "It was a case of theft that required some of the good jungle training Uncle Sam laid on me. I stayed to be with Star."

"But you don't look any older than when I saw you in the sixties!"

"I am older, Alex. I took special long-life treatments that will keep me at this age, biologically, until I die. With luck, that won't be for another century or more."

We crested the hill and I see what I assume is our goal. Oscar stops for a moment, unslings a water bottle, takes a slug, and gives it to me. "Just water, my friend. I'm sorry there's nothing stronger. In an hour we'll be at the manor house."

Seeing Tam and Palina running down the

hill, he turns to start off again. But I grab his arm. There's one question that can wait no longer.

"Oscar, I can accept everything, all that you've told me. The gates, the Twenty Universes, as implausible as it all sounds I can buy it. But there's one thing I don't understand. Why am I here? Why was I brought here?"

"Oh, that," he laughs out loud. "Oh, nobody *has* told you yet, have they? You see, Alex, my friend, I needed someone I knew, someone I could trust, someone not from this world, or Center, the ruling world, someone with all your peculiar qualifications."

"What on earth for?"

"Why, my boy," he says, even though I look a good fifteen years older than he. "To save the whole ball of wax—all Twenty Universes." He drapes his powerful right arm on my shoulder.

"You, my friend, are going to save us all."

Roll 3 D6.

If the total is less than or equal to Alex's value for Wisdom, turn to section 51.

If the total is greater than his value for Wisdom, turn to section 44.

* **41** *

The entrance hallway is enormous, easily holding the crowd that enters and mills about. The servants quickly navigate through the maze of people, offering goblets of what seems to be wine.

I pick one up and taste it—it has a dry, fruity taste. It didn't come from grapes, but it is certainly good. Jocko and Oscar are laughing and toasting each other—I assume that sooner or later they will get around to showing me a room, perhaps giving me some dry clothes.

I see Palina standing to the side, aloof and distant. We haven't said more than a few words to each other since crossing into this world. Maybe, I think, now is the time to get her side of the story.

"Nice party, come here often?"

She is not drinking. "An unfortunate necessity," she mutters. "I'd much rather get a quiet night's sleep and leave well-rested in the morning. Jocko, though, must have his celebration."

Huge double doors open and a phalanx of servants enters—chambermaids, one for each guest. "Easy . . . I mean, Oscar didn't have

Section 41

much to say about our adventure. Just that we have to kill Bad William."

Palina looks at me—and for a second it gives me a chill. It's like she is looking at a dead man.

"No, Alex. While Tam and I will be helping you, it will fall to you to kill Bad William. I just hope that your tricks stowed away in Tam's bag are good enough to interest the madman."

"Maybe I should just take a rain check on the whole deal. If you'd just direct me to the nearest gate out of here—"

"If you tried to leave, Oscar would have you killed. Now, if you'll excuse me, the chambermaids are here."

And sure enough, a petite but buxom young woman dressed in a starched white and tan dress is by my side with an armful of towels.

"*T-Vamma ako l'nika*," she says, and I look to Palina for help.

"She wants to show you to your room . . ."

I smile, looking forward to a hot shower, a meal, and some more of this Nevian wine.

Tomorrow, I think cavalierly, can take care of itself.

Turn to section 49.

* **42** *

All of a sudden, the long day's activities hit me like the worst of jet lag. The idea of falling right into bed seems deliciously attractive.

I wave to Oscar, over at the other side of the big dining room, and gesture that I am going to sleep.

He smiles, and waves me away.

Once in my room, I fall into my bed wishing I could sleep for a week.

Turn to section 55.

* **43** *

What the hell, I think. It's not like I was running around trying to seduce all the females in the Doral's rather extended family. This buxom lady obviously knows what she wants. And surprisingly, after all the wine, so do I. I give Oscar a sheepish grin (hoping he has enough clout to smooth over any difficulties with Jocko), but I'm amazed to see both of them raise their goblets to me in salute.

Well, when in Rome, I think. It's always fun to learn new customs from different lands.

She is laughing wholeheartedly by now, tugging me along. (I'm sure she has told me her name by now but it blended into all the other mumbo jumbo words.)

I'm just about to turn down the long hallway at the top of the stairs when I feel, really feel, someone's eyes on me. Imagining the lady's husband back from the tractor convention in Kansas City, I turn.

It's Palina. And the look on her face speaks, momentarily at least, of disappointment.

But I'm yanked away rather quickly, and it will be an hour or two of healthy exercise (including some new twists that I thought were impossible) before blessed sleep claims my sweaty and overtired body.

Turn to section 55.

∗ **44** ∗

Back in Southeast Asia, I liked Gordon. But I knew that I could never really trust him. He was juggling too many balls in the air at one time for anyone to really depend upon him. I wasn't surprised to hear that he ended up in the Riviera in lieu of Seattle.

And I'm not surprised to learn that he was married to an empress.

I just hope that we are good enough friends from the old days that he'll give me the straight story on what's going on here.

As fantastic as that story might turn out to be.

Turn to section 56.

* **45** *

Tam seems lost, standing near the entrance, just a kid now among so many adults. She has even stopped popping her gum, and I surmise that such an earthly activity might be frowned upon by her father.

I walk over to her.

"It sounds like we have ourselves an adventure tomorrow?"

She looks at me and grins. "It sure sounds that way," she answers.

I detect that she knows something that I'm not privy to. "You sound like you've got a secret. C'mon, out with it."

She looks around, making sure that we are out of earshot of everyone. Huge oaken doors open and a phalanx of what looks like chambermaids enters.

"Now don't let Pal know I told you, promise?"

"Scouts honor."

"But my dad says we're to leave you once you are at Bad William's castle. Your only way out of this will be if you kill him . . . or he kills you."

Section 45

I look at Oscar, and he signals me to come over and grab a goblet of wine.

"If you confront Palina before she leaves, you can make her stay." Tam looks up at me and gives me a knowing wink. "You'll have an easier time with Bad William if you have our help."

"Thanks, sprout." I rustle her closely cropped hair. "I owe you a case of Double Bubble."

"You sure do."

I walk over to Oscar, and grab a goblet of wine.

"To magic and Bad William's demise," he proposes, and Jocko repeats it in the local lingo.

"And to a million dollars," I add.

"Oh, yes, a million dollars," Oscar says, laughing.

I drink the goblet of fruity wine in one great gulp.

Turn to section 49.

* **46** *

Roll 3 D6.

If the total is less than or equal to Alex's value for Strength, turn to section 47.

If the total is greater than his value for Strength, turn to section 58.

* **47** *

Fear, as I may have mentioned before, is a wonderful motivator. The dragon wastes no time getting up off the forest floor and coming after me. But I move as fast as my little feet can carry me, and I don't look back.

But once it's up and moving, it's amazing how fast the dragon can get that great body running.

I think I can smell its foul breath hitting my back (a revolting mixture of rat fur and Elizabeth, New Jersey). I'm sure he (or she) will soon be in a position to bite my head off like the top of a celery stick.

But why isn't it using its flame breath to torch me?

I pull out my sword.

Then Palina and Tam are there.

"Turn, Alex," Palina screams. "Turn and fight!"

Now that the odds have improved, I spin around.

Turn to section 70.

* **48** *

Somehow, I trust Tam most of all. She seems terribly honest in that charming and sometimes hurtful way that kids can be.

Despite the fact that she is Oscar's daughter, I think it might be worth trying to talk with her about our upcoming adventure.

If Alex talks with Tam, turn to section 45.

If Alex talks to Palina, turn to section 41.

If he decides to just enjoy the festivities, turn to section 49.

* 49 *

I've been to parties where I didn't know anyone, somehow suffering through the interminable chips and dips until it was polite to go home. In fact, right after my wife left me—informing me that only a fool would try to make a career out of magic—a number of my friends invited me to such parties. I ended up standing in the corner though, thinking that whoever created the cocktail party had a rather limited idea of fun.

This bash, though, is entirely different. My room, up on the second floor of the manor house, is a large bedroom, rough and rustic but mighty big. There are some clean clothes laid out on the bed—garments made from a very soft kind of leather (made, I later learned, from the tanned hides of a local version of a pig).

And there is a shower, which removes the last traces of swamp muck from my now-aching body.

By the time I get downstairs, a Rabelaisian feast of major proportions is going on. The language being spoken seems like those weird sounds made by a record being played backward. Oscar gives me a wave, but stays by Jocko's side, matching him goblet for goblet, while a small brass band pumps out some thumping music.

Everyone looks at me (I smile back), but I soon find that no one else speaks English. After a while, I sort of settle into a pattern of walking around, sipping the local wine (which did much to put me at ease) and tasting chunks of meat and fruit from the overloaded platters.

I don't see Tam at all. Perhaps she's already in bed, but I look for Palina.

I'm on my third goblet, when she comes down the stairs. She's exchanged her earthly attire for something truly out of this world. It's a pale blue floor-length gown that appears to float about her. It seems to catch every gentle curve of her body and at times, I swear, I can see right through it. It looks like it has been made for her.

And I'm not alone looking at her. The general din goes down a few notches when Palina walks down the steps.

Oscar walks past me, heading in the direction that I imagine the W.C. to be. "It's her mother's dress, Alex. It always worked for her, too," he says as he passes.

I nod, unwilling to take my eyes off her. I hope that she'll come over to talk with me, but she is soon surrounded by a gaggle of local bumpkins, all of whom apparently know her.

Disgruntled, I turn away and nurse my regrets with the local wine.

Section 49

If Alex goes to sleep now, turn to section 42.

If Alex stays at the party, turn to section 50.

* **50** *

I'm bone-tired, but it doesn't seem polite to just crawl upstairs while the party is very much in high gear.

I do spot an empty seat near the corner and I head directly for it. Sitting, at this point, will be much better than standing.

My mouth is open in mid-yawn, when suddenly there is someone standing very close to me. I think she's one of Jocko's daughters (or perhaps his granddaughter). Her long brown hair is pinned up behind her, and she is wearing a low-cut blouse that barely covers her natural resources. She says something, but I assume she is talking to someone else. Then she repeats it.

"*Ala t'lila k'naash, vra?*"

Sure, honey, I think, anything you say. I smile, dopily. Her face grows confused, almost a bit angry. I look around for Oscar or Palina to translate, but they are both occupied. I give her my best smile, trying to marshal the modest amount of charm I have. She seems to relax a bit, and grabs my hand, pulling me to my feet.

Section 50

"*T'lila, vra?*"

"No speakee the lingo, chop chop?" I say, and she giggles. Soon it's clear where she is dragging me. This little farmland cupcake is dragging me upstairs . . . I notice Oscar glance in my direction, followed by our host, and I imagine their smiles fading away.

I am, I think, perhaps about to commit my first major faux pas on this odd world.

I give her hand a squeeze.

If Alex continues upstairs, turn to section 43.

If Alex pulls away and rejoins the party, turn to section 53.

* **51** *

Easy Gordon, I think, now consort to the empress and buccaneer of the Twenty Universes.

Yet, I have this distinct memory of his being less than forthright in his dealings, whether it was with the U.S. Army or some friends in an all-night poker game.

He may be my only supply of information on this world, but it's a source that will bear watching.

Even as I listen to him, I try to figure out just what he might not be telling me.

Add +1 to Alex's Intelligence value for the remainder of his adventure.

Then turn to section 56.

* 52 *

I pull out my sword, a bit nonplussed to be handling a heavy, twin-bladed item instead of my nifty cutlass.

The dragon, though, seems unimpressed.

It rears back, like some monstrous puppy dog about to grind its master into the dirt.

Its eyes are wide open, angry, and hungry.

It opens its mouth.

DRAGON
To hit hero: 11   To be hit: 12   Hit points: 14
Damage: 1 D6   Damage with sword: 1 D6 +1
The dragon will attempt to use its flame breath but nothing happens.

If Alex's hit roll should ever be a six or less, turn to section 64.

If Alex's hit points are down to 0, turn to section 29.

If the dragon is killed, turn to section 65. After the third round of combat, turn to section 61.

* **53** *

I jerk my hand back. No reason to get the old Doral upset. I'm a guest, and the last thing I need is to insult the old boy by bedding down his daughter.

I slip down the steps away from her, holding out my hand in apology.

Then I hear the roar.

The room falls silent as Jocko's booming, barrel-chested baritone cuts through the festive air.

Wrong move, I think.

He leaps up on the table and draws out an obscenely large sword.

"Now wait a minute, Doral, my lord," but one look at Jocko's red, inflamed face tells me that words will do nothing to mollify him.

He jumps down to the floor and brings back his sword.

Obviously I've insulted him *and* his daughter (or granddaughter) by not marching upstairs for some dalliance. Go figure.

His arm muscles flex and I suck in a breath. (Last one, I think.)

"*Amech!*"

Then, like a sweet angel of mercy, Palina is

there. In an instant she has stepped between
and relieved some nearby party-goer of his
blade.

"*Amech,* Jocko. *T'knila* Alex *varota nish.*"

"Right on, girl," I whisper.

Jocko eyes me carefully.

"Alex, you have done the house of Milord
Doral't Giuk and Dorali great insult. He of-
fered you his finest granddaughter and you
turned her down."

"So what now, princess? Any way to mollify
the old bear?"

"Maybe. Bow slightly to the Doral, and
slowly, and then remount the steps and take
her hand and kiss it. Raise her hand high
above your head for everyone to see."

"Are you su—"

"Move, Alex." And I do, first making nice
with the bow and then going up the steps. The
girl tries, quite naturally, to pull her hand
away, but I hold it tight, all the time keeping a
grin on my face.

Jocko watches the proceedings carefully, but
finally a broad smile fills his face and he lowers
his sword.

"*T'knila* Alex *ara,*" he booms at me.

Palina translates . . . "Enjoy the pleasures of
my house," she whispers.

"Thank you, Doral," I say. At once the party
starts up again, like a record suddenly coming
to life on a turntable.

"Enjoy," says Palina dryly. "But get some
sleep. We leave early."

It's a good two hours, though, of exertion

Section 53

and sweat, before sleep finally claims my pained and overtired body.

Turn to section 55.

* **54** *

Dragons are smart animals, I figure. Sure they are. They have treasure hoards and they like riddles. (Or, I wonder, is that some other kind of mythical creature?)

"Hello, friend," I say with all the aplomb of a robber trying to calm an attacking Doberman pinscher. "I just happen to be moving through this lovely woods with my friends . . ."

Too late it occurs to me that if the people around here don't know English, then what are the chances that this overgrown gila monster will understand it?

None.

Its tail swishes around behind me, expending no more effort than necessary to knock me off my feet and plop me in front of the dragon's mouth. I'm now in position to see it raise its right front claw and begin to lower it down upon me.

I reach, a bit tardily perhaps, for my sword.

The dragon gets the first attack, thereafter all combat is simultaneous.

Turn to section 52.

* **55** *

"Alex, get up. They are ready for us to leave."

I blink awake, and the blurry image of Palina dressed in leather pants and vest comes into focus.

"I let you sleep as long as possible."

"Thanks." She starts for the door. "Say, Palina, what do you say we leave a bit later on today, after lunch, or maybe . . ."

"Now, Alex. Unless you want Oscar to haul you out of bed."

Acknowledging the inevitable, I take a quick shower, dress in my Robin Hood gear, and go downstairs.

Where everyone is, indeed, waiting. Oscar, Jocko, and his assorted tribe, the fieldhands—with their wide-brimmed hats and pitchforks in hand—waiting beside some very strange animals.

That look a bit like horses. I mean, they have some kind of saddle on. But each animal has eight legs, fitted rather intricately into a harness, and the heads on the animals make them look like sleepy-eyed dachshunds.

Oscar comes up to me and grabs me by the shoulders.

"A lot depends upon you, Alex," he says quietly. "I'd come if all hell wasn't breaking loose on Center. I must protect Star. But you . . ." he says, his eyes catching the early morning light, "must protect my Tam. Sometimes she doesn't know when she's in over her head."

"Unlike me," I answer. I think once again of announcing my dispensability in this particular task, but such a thought ends when Jocko starts proclaiming something that sounds like poetry.

"It's in your honor," Oscar explains. "It recounts your battle with the alligators and the constructs, and predicts your future victory against Bad William. I'm afraid that, when he's done, you'll have to answer with a bit of verse yourself."

Since most of my reading tends toward Travis McGee books and police procedurals, I don't have a lot of material to draw on.

"Alex," Oscar says quietly, "your turn."

I smile at everyone. Then I launch into my one, and only, stanza . . .

> *"As I was going up the stair*
> *I met a man who wasn't there.*
> *He wasn't there again today*
> *I wish to God he'd go away."*

Jocko seems to consider a moment, then claps his meaty hands together. "Up you go, friend," Oscar says, indicating the nearest octopoid mount. He helps hoist me up. "These levers," he says, pointing to a pair of sticks on the right and left of the saddle, "make the beast go faster or slower. Just take it easy when you first start."

Then Oscar backs away. Tam is already on her mount, waving at the crowd who are cheering and performing a strange twisted sort of curtsy—a Nevian custom, apparently.

"All set, Alex?" Palina asks.

"If you say so."

"Then give everyone a big smile and a wave and let's hit the road."

I do as ordered, and amazingly enough my horse-thing moves smoothly ahead.

It isn't long before we come to a road actually made of yellow, hexagonal bricks.

"Is this Munchkin land?" I ask.

"What's a Munchkin?" Tam responds, deadpan.

"There are no creatures called Munchkins in this world," Palina explains. "I doubt there'll be any call for us to go to that universe."

"That's too bad. I've always wanted an honorary membership in the Lullaby League."

My attempts at humor do nothing to dispel the gloom that seems to hang over Palina and Tam. They obviously know something I don't, and it's perhaps my good fortune that I'm in the dark.

But I do have one question to ask.

"Palina, there's one thing I don't quite understand." I pull on my animal's throttle and soon I am next to Palina. "If Bad William sent constructs to warn me away, scare me, how can I slip into his city without being discovered?"

Tam giggles, an oddly bloodthirsty sound for one so young. Palina gives her a glare, then answers. "The constructs—there were two— were following us. But until we actually made contact with you, there's no way they'd know you were a recruit."

"And after?"

"They did their best to stop you."

"But what's to keep them from telling Bad William about me?"

Tam giggles again. "Because," Palina says, sighing, "we made sure they didn't live to tell him. Nobody knows about you, Alex, and we plan to keep it that way."

"Oh."

It isn't long before we turn off the road and enter the woods. The trees resemble earthly trees, except for the tremendously broad leaves that block almost all the sunlight.

"We'll avoid dragon country this way," Palina says.

"Sounds good to me," I reply.

"But what about the weather?" Tam asks. I detect more than a hint of nervousness in her voice.

"Calm weather is predicted for the mountains," Palina answers curtly. "We don't have anything to worry about."

"But if it changes, we could be—"

"It won't change, Tam. Now get to the rear, and keep your eyes open."

Palina charges ahead, leaving me alone. The mountains, our destination, are completely blocked by deep woods. If it is dark and gloomy now, I can't imagine what it will be like at night.

We stop for lunch in a small clearing. One of the huge trees has been felled in a storm, and there is a small hole in the forest roof to let light through.

The beasts help themselves to the water, and I join them. Palina digs out some bread and greenish fruit. It tastes like very sweet string beans, nice and chewy.

After eating, Tam takes her sword out and starts rubbing a stone back and forth on it, while Palina gives the animals something to eat.

I get up and stretch and start to walk away from camp.

"Stay nearby, Alex."

"Oh, I will, princess. Just want to stretch my legs."

It's strange walking through a forest that is similar to one on earth, but with small differences. The bark on the trees is smooth and leathery, almost like the skin of an orange. When the leaves fall, they dry to a rigid, brittle shape. Here and there, there are patches of fine grass that look like chives. And once, I swear, I see a two-headed bird.

(Only later will I learn that it is in the rodent family, something like a bat.)

But I almost walk into the dragon. I'm looking left and right, not realizing that I'm out of sight of camp. I guess I take the dark, almost purplish shape ahead of me for a huge chunk of granite.

When I finally look up and see it, that familiar rounded shape from storybooks and legend (probably the gates were used in days of lore), it's too late to dash away.

Dragons, I will later learn, are smart. And though they are big, ferocious, fire-breathing monsters, the Nevians accept them as part of the planet's food chain. They eat the dog-sized rats, who in turn eat the hogs who eat the farmers' crops.

The dragons help keep things in check.

Only now, it's me who seems about to enter the food chain.

Decide what Alex should do.

If he tries to run away as fast as his legs can carry him, turn to section 46.

If he draws his sword, turn to section 52.

If he attempts to reason with the dragon, turn to section 54.

* **56** *

"Twenty plus one," he says, his face gone grim. It turns out that there was another universe discovered, a strangely beautiful place with odd creatures and a science that makes Wonderland look positively pedestrian. There's no problem in that, Oscar tells me. The problem is someone named Bad William.

"*Bad* William?"

Oscar gives me a condescending smile. "You see, Alex, William was one of the possible candidates for emperor, a super intelligence with an excellent facility in what you'd call 'magic.' But it's really just another kind of science. Star didn't have a chance at the empress's slot with William in the running.

"But then they found the genetic foul-up . . . some kind of mental disorder that indicated that William would snap under the intense pressure of training. William faded back to oblivion. At least, that's what everyone thought."

The large manor house is quite close now. Tam and Palina break into a run and dash toward it. Tremendous fields stretch east and west, containing what looks like row after row of corn. The fieldhands are dressed in simple wraparound garments, their heads protected from the sun by broad-brimmed hats. It's a scene out of a bucolic Durer etching.

People are coming out of the main house, dressed more colorfully, and it seems like some kind of celebration is about to begin.

"Easy, go on with your story."

"'Oscar,' friend Alex. No one knows me here by any other name. Everyone knows the name Oscar, though not everyone will give you such a pleasant reception as we are about to have. We shall eat tonight."

"The story?"

"William pursued the scientific arts on his own, becoming extraordinarily proficient. But his discovery of another universe, unknown to the old emperors, gave him access to technology we knew nothing about and, what's worse, an ability to influence events in all the other universes."

"Surely you could send armies and attack his world."

"Sure we could. And they'd be just as quickly destroyed. It's a world completely controlled by Bad William. He started turning the peoples of the other universes against the empress, partly because they were scared, partly because he was helping them. Every emperor and empress is ultimately assassinated—it's just the way things work—but Star was getting primed to be bumped off a good hundred years ahead of her time. Something had to be done."

"I still don't see how I fit into the picture."

A burly old fellow followed by a festive gathering of servants, children, and wenches of Falstaffian proportions advances on us. I'm intrigued, excited, and mostly hungry. But I grab Oscar and turn him toward me.

"Why me?"

"Believe it or not, Alex, the tricks you do would attract the attention of Bad William. Still do that saw-a-woman-in-half number?"

"I've improved it."

"Yes, Bad William will want to check your act out up close. Then, all you have to do is kill him."

"When does all this fun begin for us?"

Oscar laughs. "I'm afraid I won't be able to come, Alex. If I entered the gate to his planet, he'd know it in ten seconds. No, Tam and Palina will accompany you. They are gifted psi-coms, psychic communicators. Palina and Tam are Star's daughters, and Tam can also get some readings about events still to come. But take care of her, Alex, because she's also my daughter."

"Oscar! *T'klinia voorsht vramach*!"

The burly fellow has his arms extended, seemingly reaching around to crush us to his ample body.

"Alex, may I present a scoundrel and a scalawag, and one of my best friends, the Milord Doral't Giuk Dorali. But I call him Jocko."

"Jocko," he laughs, squeezing Oscar until the air in his lungs makes a wheezing sound as it escapes. Then he turns his attentions to me. "Tonight, we are celebrating until dawn," he says in broken English.

"That's when you leave," Oscar mumbles quietly. "I've been teaching him English . . . pretty good, huh?"

To my chagrin, there seems to be no choice in the matter.

I follow the crowd into the manor house, eyeing a wench or two who seem to return my glances.

Roll 3 D6.

If the total is less than or equal to Alex's value for Intelligence, turn to section 48.

If the total is greater than his value for Intelligence, read below.

Decide what Alex will do.

If he decides to try to speak with Palina about the morning's quest, turn to section 41.

If he decides to speak with Tam about her father and Bad William, turn to section 45.

If he simply relaxes and enjoys the festivities, turn to section 49.

* **57** *

Science was not my forte in high school. But even I know that raising my sword to this thing will only send its probably deadly voltage right through my body.

If Alex dodges, turn to section 67.

If Alex tries his sword anyway, turn to section 60.

* **58** *

I start to run, hoping that fear will inject just the right amount of adrenaline to get me away from the overgrown lizard.

But, as fate would have it, I slip on one of the broad leaves littering the forest floor, and by the time I'm up and running again, the dragon and I are eyeball to eyeball.

With the greatest reluctance (and absolutely no confidence) I take out my sword.

Turn to section 52.

* **59** *

The cold and the ice give me an idea. If this thing is electricity the way we have it back home, it can be grounded by water.

And what's ice but frozen water?

All I have to do is dodge it a couple of times, let it hit the wall and ground itself.

Maybe . . .

Turn to section 71.

Add +1 to any Dexterity rolls while Alex is dealing with the Living Lightning.

* **60** *

I raise my sword as if I were facing a buccaneer about to board my man-of-war.

"No, Alex!" I hear Palina scream from inside the cave. "Not your *sword!*"

Right, I think, dumbly looking at the sword and the ball of lightning coming at me. Fighting electricity with a piece of metal is probably a bad idea.

I try to hurl the heavy sword backward and dodge Mr. G.E. before I get toasted.

Roll 3 D6.

If the total is less than or equal to Alex's value for Dexterity, turn to section 74.

If the total is greater than Alex's value for Dexterity, turn to section 62.

* **61** *

Things are looking more than grim when I notice two familiar figures moving toward me. Palina and Tam have their swords out and ready.

And not a moment too soon.

Turn to section 70.

* **62** *

It should be easy—twist to the left and let the lack of gravity lift me away from the lightning.

But I don't run fast enough, and I sniff a weird smell like ozone only seconds before the lightning creature hits.

At the last moment, before I become human toast, I think I hear Palina call out to me.

And that almost makes it all worthwhile.

Almost . . .

Turn to section 29.

* **63** *

The first jab misses and sends weird sparks flying all over the cave. Tam screams and hugs Palina. When the creature rears back for its second attack, Tam reaches down and tosses a rock at the thing's head.

The rock, needless to say, disintegrates in midair.

A bad sign of what's in store for me.

Then the creature leaps right at me, and I think I smell my body hair being singed.

But the wall behind me has melted a bit after its first blow, and the creature hits the slimy wet wall. With a horrible yowl, it seems to spark more brightly, then fade, the color and light being drawn from it, leaving only a pale outline of the creature.

Then, there is absolutely nothing.

I turn away and tentatively touch the wall, letting my finger run along the shiny surface.

"When's the next one due?" I ask Palina.

Palina and Tam run over and encircle me, squeezing. "Hey, guys, I know you love me, but just take it easy."

"What killed it?" Tam asks.

"The water, sprout. Water and electricity don't mix."

"C'mon," Palina says to Tam. "Lie down and get some rest." She pulls blankets out of the ever-bountiful backpack. (I just *have* to get one of those things.) "I've set a ward so we can get some sleep."

She sits by Tam awhile, in the darkness, gently caressing her forehead, singing something softly in the native tongue that sounds wonderfully soothing.

I take my blanket and go to the other corner of the cave.

I have just curled up, ready to try and get some sleep, when Palina is there next to me.

"Tam's asleep," she whispers. "This has been very hard for her."

I turn toward Palina, not really able to see her face in the almost total gloom. "Couldn't she see the attack coming, I mean if she has powers?"

"Her powers are erratic, and they work best with people. She'll help you once we meet Bad William."

I wait, feeling she is going to say something else.

But she doesn't. Her hand reaches out and she pulls herself close to me. "I was worried about you, Alex. I was scared."

"So was I."

And we kiss. The best kiss I've had since making out in my dad's old Buick. Rich, rubbery, and loaded with the hope of thrills deferred to another, more private, time.

Section 63

And best of all, I just barely keep myself from telling her that I love her.

I awake to find Palina gone from my side. She and Tam are near the small cave's entrance, unrolling the rope. My body feels like a side of beef hanging in a meat freezer. I'm numb, and every movement brings some pain.

"Good morning. There's some tea, in that mug," Palina says cheerily, "and Tam still has fruit in her backpack."

"I bet she does." I look over at Tam. She seems oddly quiet. "Good morning, sprout. Sleep okay?"

She nods, but keeps her head down.

I've barely finished the tea (a rich herbal concoction that tastes more like broth) when Palina gives orders to move out.

Going down the mountain is tricky indeed. Now, in a crazy way, we are fighting the lack of gravity, and it's strange to struggle to climb down.

But the day is sunny—not a cloud in the sky—and we make quick work of the other side of the mountain. The gate, which I'm learning can appear in the most peculiar places, is right at the foot of the mountain.

Once again Palina and Tam perform their ritual, carving lines and runes into the dirt, and once again they both become entirely serious as we take positions for our passage.

I feel the same light-headed feeling as before, and then we are someplace else.

It's beautiful. The surrounding trees are

heavy and lush with the fullness of summer. And there must be twenty different shades of green, from a dark, almost blackish hue to a pale, wispy grass-green. Bright birds with long tail feathers and curved beaks dart excitedly overhead, squawking noisily at the intrusion.

"It's gorgeous," I say. "Absolutely wonderful."

I almost don't notice Tam pulling an arsenal out of her backpack.

"Hey, what are you doing, sprout?"

"We're in a place where we can use guns," Palina explains. "And this—" She slips two small plugs into my ears, "will help you understand any of the languages here, and most of the people you meet will also be able to understand you."

Tam meanwhile is snapping together parts of a gun. Then she hands it to me.

"You fire it just like an Earth weapon," she demonstrates. "Just keep the safety latch on while we're hiking."

I take it from her—an honest-to-goodness ray gun.

"We're going to need this?" I ask.

"Possibly. This is a new universe for us . . . there's a lot we don't know," Palina says.

The gun seems incongruous. I won't be surprised to see a snow-white unicorn standing alone, patting the ground in challenge to our intrusion.

Instead, we meet the Mischief Men. They don't call themselves that. But we have trouble pronouncing their real names, and by the time we get done with them, the name "Mischief Men" seems more than apt.

The first one flies overhead just as we start in the direction (on the map, at least) of Bad William's town. At first, I think it's a bird, some kind of squat turkey or duck. But then two or three of them fly right in front of us, hover a moment, and then whiz away.

"What are they?" I ask Palina, who just shakes her head.

"They're cute," Tam says.

As if they hear her, they reappear, only now there are nearly a dozen of them. They are roly-poly little fellows about the size of a basketball, with beanbag heads, tiny, almost babylike hands, and foot-long tails that move around like propellers.

They float in front of us, grinning dopily, their tongues lolling out of their mouths.

"I want one," Tam says.

"We're not too sure they're not dangerous, sprout."

"Their bodies have to be filled mostly with air," Palina observes. "Otherwise—"

"Quite correct," the Mischief Man closest to us says. And the others repeat it, doing a 360-degree turn in midair.

"We're glad you can talk," I say, smiling.

"So are we," the Mischief Man giggles and the rest of the squadron responds in kind.

"We're going to Bad William's town," Palina says.

They disappear, scattering like dandelion

seeds in a summer breeze. They obviously have no affection for Bad William.

Slowly, one by one, the Mischief Men glide back to us.

"You must not go this way, no, no, right into a trap," the leader giggles. "You must go *that* way." He points in a direction that will take us off the trail, down the valley. We probably can still get to the town, but it will take longer.

"Why not straight ahead?" Palina demands.

"Bad William has set traps." More annoying giggles. "He will catch you."

I turn to Palina. "What do you think?"

"Tam," she says, "get out the reader and check the scroll on this universe."

Tam brings out a clear piece of plastic. At the very top she fastens what looks like a piece of film. "Here, Pal, but I don't think there's anything about these guys."

Palina takes the box and slides the scroll into it, and it flashes the collected information about this universe. Then she turns it off with a sigh.

"Nothing on them. So what do you think we should do?"

The Mischief Men are still hovering in front of us, expectantly, apparently enjoying the quandary they have put us in.

If Alex recommends following the Mischief Men's suggestion, turn to section 76.

If Alex suggests continuing on the trail to the town, turn to section 69.

* **64** *

The dragon raises first his left, and then the right front leg, a lizard pugilist trying to make a knockout swipe.

Even in the gloom I can see the dragon's oversize canines with bits of collected gunk stuck to them. (And I wonder will I soon be getting a closer look.)

Being eaten, I figure, has to be the absolutely worst way to go.

It opens and closes its mouth in anticipation of chow time.

I step forward, surprising both the dragon and myself. It's up, exposing the whitish-pink skin of its underbelly. It looks decidedly easier to puncture it there than on the pebbly rough armor that surrounds it everywhere else.

I pause just a second, trying to get a fix on my point of attack. Then I run forward.

Turn to section 65.

* **65** *

The dragon's scream tells me I have done it major damage. But I'm still surprised when I see it stop dead in its tracks and keel over onto the leafy forest floor.

"Well done, Alex," Palina says.

"Couldn't have done better myself," Tam chimes in, running ahead to climb on the dragon's body.

"Careful, Tam," I yell. "It might not be dead."

"Come down," Palina orders, and Tam reluctantly gets off the creature, like a kid being made to leave a jungle gym.

Palina walks over to the dragon and rams her sword into its gullet. Then she cuts a fine line, leading down to its midsection.

"What in the world are you—"

She uses her sword and a trusty knife to pry open the dragon's flaps of skin.

"Just as I thought," she says, getting up.

"What do you mean?"

She turns to me. "Did it occur to you to wonder why the dragon didn't just shoot its fire breath at you?"

Section 65

"No. I mean, I thought maybe it was a made-up story, about breathing fire and all."

"They make their fire by belching forth a gas from their stomach, quite like methane, and ignite it by clicking together the two teeth on the side of the jaw. So why didn't it use it on you?"

"Okay, I'll bite. Why?"

"Because it has been poisoned, which explains why it's so far away from its normal range. And why you had such an easy time killing it. The poor thing was delirious."

Tam has made her way back up to the dragon and is clambering up its spiky tail.

"But who'd want to do that?"

Palina draws her sword back and forth across a leaf, cleaning it. And then she slides it back into its sheath.

"Bad William. Get rid of the dragons, and the rats get out of control. Soon there'd be so many of them they'd be snatching babies out of cribs. The whole planet would get angry, turning against the empress. Bad William could step in and become their savior."

"What a bad guy."

Palina rolls her eyes. "Don't worry, Alex. You'll get plenty of opportunity to learn just how *bad* William can be."

"Hope he likes magic," I mumble, but Palina is already heading back to where our mounts are tied up.

Turn to section 72.

* **66** *

I'm a pool person. I like my water blue and loaded to the max with chlorine. No algae, no animals, and no murky bottom with who knows what lurking around.

Crossing this river, then, is not an activity I normally would have chosen. In fact, if it wasn't for Palina cavalierly wading across, her gun and sword both held high out of the water, I'd have pressed for a more thorough search for a bridge or a ferry boat.

The water (it is, I believe, normal everyday H_2O) is cool, and not unpleasant after the hot hike through the forest. I just could do without stepping on the muck, imagining all sorts of snaky things to be coiling and uncoiling around my feet.

Ahead, the water has reached Palina's chin.

"Too deep," I yell. "Perhaps we should go back."

"No," she answers vehemently, just about able to keep her weapons from getting wet. "It's level. We can get across if you carry Tam across the deep part."

I turn to Tam. "What do you say, sprout,

shall I hoist you on my shoulders, or do you—"

"Alex!" Tam screams. I turn around.

Now, I grew up in a small town on the Hudson. In the winter giant ice floes from the north would flow down to New York Harbor and the Atlantic Ocean. In spring, the ocean water and fresh water mix, creating a brackish mixture that combines denizens of both salt and fresh water.

But I'd never swim in it.

Not because of the PCBs. Or the garbage that people dumped in it. Or the floating pools of gasoline from the pleasure boaters.

I wouldn't swim the river because it had eels. Big, black, slimy creatures that laid their eggs in the Hudson and then migrated back to, of all places, the Sargasso sea. People said they were harmless (like my har-de-har dad who joked about them biting me, saying, "They won't eat much"), but I stayed out anyway.

Just as we should have stayed out of this river.

"Alex, don't just stand there! Do something!"

Palina is in midair, trapped in a coil of what looks like the biggest eel in the universe. It has one blackish-blue eye, and its nictitating eyelid is blinking rapidly open and shut as if not used to being above the surface of the water.

From all I can tell, Palina may be dead already. Her eyes are shut and her body just hangs in the eel's coil like a broken doll.

I have Tam's gun in the backpack, so whatever happens will depend upon me. And so far, I haven't shown any prowess in the category of combat arts.

If Alex uses the ray gun, turn to section 79.

If Alex decides to attack the eel with his sword, turn to section 77.

* **67** *

The lightning seems to be moving remarkably slowly, but then I'm not about to complain.

I try to twist away from its planned trajectory.

Roll 3 D6.

If the total is less than or equal to Alex's value for Dexterity, turn to section 74.

If the total is greater than Alex's value for Dexterity, turn to section 62.

* **68** *

One of the knights brings his flying horse up toward the left. I have him in my sight, really have him, and I fire.

Another miss.

But he isn't gunning for me. The bastard has Tam picked out.

And she doesn't even see him.

"Tam!" I yell.

He fires, and I hear her scream.

I throw my gun to the side.

"Wait!" I yell as another knight comes bearing down toward us.

"She's hit, I've got to—"

The voice that answers me is metallic, like the suit he wears.

"You surrender, varlet?"

Palina has already crawled to her sister. "Yes. Now, can I help her . . ."

The knight gets off his horse, which stays there floating while it whirrs and whines. He pulls out a sword.

"Put them in chains."

Another knight arrives with chains that look like they are more than adequate to hold King Kong.

Section 68

"How is she?" I ask Palina.

"It's a nasty wound," Palina says. "I can't stop the bleeding from her shoulder. I'll need something from the pack."

Turn to section 87.

* **69** *

I don't think that we should trust these flying basketballs, and I say that we might as well take the main trail. The Mischief Men give us an aerial salute and then vanish into the gloom.

It's obvious that this is the main road to town. We pass signs of campsites, piles of litter, and still-smoldering fires. We aren't far from the river, where the map says a bridge should be, when Tam grabs my arm tightly.

"No! I sense something ahead. This is all wrong. This is—"

Palina goes to her, holds her closely.

"What is it, Tam? What do you see?"

I make a quick decision, something I'm getting good at lately.

"Let's go," I say. "We're heading back. If Tam doesn't like it this way, that's good enough for me."

We almost run back, keeping up a steady trot, while all the time checking over our shoulders.

Then I hear it. A roaring, rumbling sound that is like the buzzing of insects, growing louder and louder.

"Ready your weapons," Palina says steadily.

"Hold it like a rifle, Alex. You should be able to feel the button near your thumb. Just make every blast count."

One of my hands holds Tam's hand, while with the other I keep the gun raised high. Oxygen debt is beginning to claim me, and the buzzing sound continues to grow.

Then I see them.

Four knights on legless horses. The horses are made of some highly polished metal, glaring even in the dim light of the forest. The knights are covered from head to foot with the same kind of armor, and their "horses" are flying right at us, powered by some kind of engine.

"What now?" I yell at Palina.

"When I give the word, take cover behind a tree and start shooting. There's only four of them."

"Lucky us. Tam, I want you to stay behind me."

"No . . ." she answers, breathlessly. "I'm a good shot and I could help."

"Now!" Palina screams.

I duck left and Tam pulls away to the right, ripping her hand out of my grip. By the time I get behind a tree, she has her weapon up and firing.

The first blast of the laserlike weapon surprises me. I brace for the recoil, but there is none. Just a high-pitched whine and the thin beam of light.

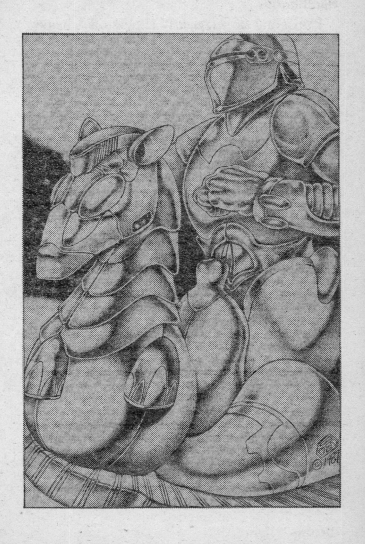

Section 69

I miss my target, neatly slicing off a heavy branch of a nearby tree. Tam is dead on, blasting one of the knights right in his breadbasket.

"Good shot, sprout," I call, and I take aim again.

BAD WILLIAM'S KNIGHTS
To be hit: 9   To hit Alex, Tam, or Palina: 6   Hit points: 7
Damage: 1 D6+1
Combat is simultaneous.
Roll to see whom each of the three surviving knights targets.
On a roll 1-2, Alex; 3-4, Palina; 5-6, Tam.
Alex, Tam, and Palina can each select a target, and they do not have to be different.

If Alex has no hit points left, turn to section 29.

If Tam is hit, turn to section 68.

If Palina is hit twice, turn to section 73.

If the knights are defeated, turn to section 75.

* **70** *

The dragon is right there, no more than ten yards away, coming at me like the IRT express into Grand Central.

"Go for the underbelly, Alex," Palina yells.

Sure, I think, if I get time to aim.

THE DRAGON
To hit Alex: 10   To be hit: 12   Hit points: 12
Damage: 1 D6   Damage: 1 D6 + 1
The dragon will attack Alex exclusively. But Tam and Palina will be trying to kill it.

For Palina to hit: 13   For Tam to hit: 12

Each one does 1 D6 of damage.

If Alex is killed, turn to section 29.

If the dragon is killed, turn to section 64.

* 71 *

The creature seems to glide toward me, crackling as it steps on the cave floor.

"Help me, Palina, what can we do?"

"I . . . I don't know, Alex. We didn't think we'd run into anything like this."

"Just don't let it touch you, Alex," Tam yells out.

Then it moves, sending one of its flashing pincer arms right at me.

LIVING LIGHTNING
To hit Alex: 8
Damage: 2 D6
To be dodged: Roll 3 D6 against Alex's Dexterity value.
If the Living Lightning hits, Alex can roll to dodge.
If it then misses, it hits the icy wall behind Alex.

If it misses twice, turn to section 63.

If Alex has no hit points left, turn to section 29.

* **72** *

We camp tonight in some gloomy, secluded spot. Palina and I take turns standing watch, but outside of an occasional strange sound, it's a quiet evening. In the morning, Tam fixes us a breakfast trail mix of assorted fruits and nuts, most of which I can't identify. But it all tastes quite good. Then, we plow on, but even Tam's normal high spirits seem subdued.

Then the mountains appear. The forest gradually dwindles to smaller trees and scrubby brush.

"We're climbing," Palina announces.

Our beasts, which have so far experienced no difficulty carrying us and our gear for the whole day, are panting hard.

"The air is getting thin," Palina explains. "In a while, we'll have to leave them and continue on foot."

The closer we get to the mountains, the more disconcerted I become. They look like no mountains I've ever seen on Earth. Instead of simply rising majestically to one peak, each mountain is littered with peaks, sharp-edged cones that seem to grow like mushrooms all over it, from the very bottom to the top.

Then Tam notices the clouds.

"Good weather's been predicted," Palina says, trying to calm her sister. But I can tell she's not free from worry herself. The closer we get to the mountains, the more impossible they appear. In some spots the small, pointy outcrops completely block any possible movement up the mountainside.

We have just reached the first scattered pile of rubble when my beast makes a noisy "har-rumph" and kneels down, camellike, on the ground. I kick my heels in and work the levers back and forth, but nothing makes it get up off the ground.

"We'll have to leave them here," Palina says. "They'll return on their own once we're away."

Tam is already down, removing her back-pack from the rear of her animal. "And we won't stop for lunch. We can eat while we march."

Is it my imagination, or is Palina starting to check the sky with some regularity? Even I can see that the dark clouds are growing even darker, loitering threateningly near the very top peak.

Tam says nothing.

"The gate is just on the other side of the mountain. We can't make it before nightfall, but it should be possible to reach it by midday tomorrow."

"You know," I say to her, "if ever you feel like telling me everything you know about this adventure, please feel free. I won't mind . . . honest."

She grins. (So she *is* human, I think.)

"You have been kept in the dark a bit, haven't you, Alex?" She's looking at me now, really looking for the first time in over two days. Despite the austere cut of her clothes (and the assorted cutlery dangling from her belt) she is still somebody I'd jump off a cliff for. And I sort of feel she knows that I'm totally infatuated.

"It's like walking through one of those amusement park fun houses," I say. "You never know what's going to pop up."

"You can blame Oscar for that. Apparently, his first exposure to the Twenty Universes was piece by piece, and he felt it was the best way to get your cooperation."

"Besides," I laugh, "where else am I going to go?" Tam has stopped, just where the actual incline of the mountain begins. She's digging around in her backpack, pulling out ropes, wires, and strange metal objects. It seems hard to believe that my magic set is still in there. There seems to be no end to the amount of things her small pack can hold.

"What's all the gear for?" I ask.

"The climb," she says, throwing a coil of heavy rope over her shoulders and passing another to Palina. She takes about a half dozen of the metal clasps and gives them to Palina and me.

"I don't think we'll need these just yet," I offer. "The way up doesn't look difficult until right near the top."

"The way up," Tam says, as if explaining

sunrise and sunset to a three-year-old, "is easy. Getting down the mountain is the hard part."

"I don't understand."

Palina steps in to reduce my ignorance of the planet's peculiar physics. "The higher we go, the less pull downward there is."

"Gravity?"

"Yes, gravity. At the very top, we will have to make handholds and crawl across carefully. The sky above us is littered with skeletons of climbers who slipped and flew upward."

"And even down here?"

"It starts gradually, but we can sense it. Just make sure that you have any small items tightly fastened to your body. Once near the top, let Tam and I direct you across."

"More clouds," Tam says.

Palina glances up quickly. "Yes . . . more clouds, Tam. Now, let's get moving."

At first, the sensation makes me giddy. Every step upward becomes more and more effortless. Though warned to step carefully, I push and jump upward, sailing over three feet to a new perch.

But once, as I pull on a rock for support, it crumbles and the pieces sort of hang suspended in the air before gently floating upward. Tam is reeling out her coil of rope. A hammer appears from her magical backpack, and she fastens the metal disks to the rock and strings the rope through them.

"Just hold onto the rope, twist your hands around it, and keep your belt-clip attached to it," she orders.

"Yes," I say, surprised at the thinness of my own voice. This is getting a bit nerve-wracking —like being in space with no rocket pack.

"Slow down, Tam!" Palina yells. "Make sure the rope is secure."

"Yes, Pal," she calls back, but I can see why she is hurrying. The clouds are almost black now. Night is a good couple of hours away, but already it is black and overcast. They're probably worried about the rain, or maybe hail.

"Hey," I say, turning back to Palina. "Won't the rain fall up too . . . we won't have to worry about that."

"Rain clouds are different . . . they are attracted to the ground. It's more like dew falling. These are mountain clouds."

"And mountain clouds," Tam yells out, "means Living Lightning."

"Living Lightning! What's Living . . ."

"Tam!" Palina screams.

I turn to look at the spot where Tam should be. But she's gone, already drifting gently out into space, over the mountain and slowly moving upward.

"Oh, no!" Palina yells. "I'll never be able to reach her."

But I can. Can, that is, if I unclip my belt and jump off the mountain with the rope held in my hands.

Tam is looking right at me. She knows I'm the only one who can save her.

"Hang on, kid, Uncle Alex is coming after you." The belt-clip sticks a moment, and I have to press down as hard as I can to undo it.

Section 72

"Give me more rope," I tell Palina.

"Not too much of a push off, Alex. If you get too much momentum you'll lose hold of the rope."

Tam is drifting farther away, perhaps even out of range of the rope. I have to jump right away.

I leap, and I immediately know it was too strong. I'm 133 pounds of accelerated mass, and all that is going to stop me from moving is my hand holding onto the rope.

I don't think I'm going to be able to do it. (Imagine dropping off a three-story building and holding onto a single strand of rope to stop your fall. Get the picture?)

My fist closes tight. The rope snaps. My hand slips an inch, two inches, burning and biting into my palm. Another inch, and my eyes water from the pain. My right arm feels like it has been pulled out from its socket.

But I hold on.

"Tam, reach for me."

She's just above me, and she stretches outward, but to no avail.

"Damn," I say. "It's not long enough." And she is still moving away.

Tam looks like she might cry.

Crazily, I start kicking at the air, doing some kind of frog kick to get just a bit closer. After a few moments of ridiculous movement, it works.

My hand closes around Tam's, and I pull her close, hugging her to me, and then she cries.

"Okay, Palina, pull us back, but gently. I don't want to lose hold."

Palina reels us in, but I rest my chin on Tam's closely cropped hair as she heaves against me. It's the first time I've seen the plucky kid scared.

I feel the mountain bump against my back, and then Palina pulls Tam from me and clips her to the rope.

"I told you you were going too fast," she yells, through her tears, kissing Tam's forehead, rubbing her hair. "You were rushing and nearly got yourself killed."

"But the clouds—"

"Yes," Palina says. "The clouds . . ."

She turns to me. "Thank you." And then she leans forward and kisses me.

"That was a brave thing to do, Alex. I'll never forget it."

"Shucks, ma'am, 'tweren't nothin'." But Palina's confused look tells me she's never seen a John Ford western.

Now Tam takes up the center position, while I bring up the rear. Palina had hoped to get well over the other side of the mountain before nightfall. Now, it seems, we will be lucky to be just over the crest before dark.

Gravity is almost nonexistent. If it wasn't so dangerous, you could simply slide along the rope, gliding upward. But it *is* dangerous, and we proceed cautiously, making sure the ropes are firmly attached and the clamps well hammered into the granitelike stone.

Section 72

Near the top, I feel the hair on my head and arms stand straight up.

"Electricity," I say. "Are we in any danger of—"

"Keep moving," Palina shouts back. "We will be safer if we can get over the top."

So even when it turns dusk and we are unable to tell the early night sky from the clouds, we keep moving. I cross the top of the mountain—a smooth, almost level place with no sense of relief or excitement. We have to keep moving.

But then it is too dark to continue, and Palina calls a halt.

"There's a pocket here where we can settle in."

"A pocket?" I ask Tam. "What's that?"

"It's like a cave, except it has some pull. If it's big enough, we should have enough gravity so we don't float away."

Palina is waiting for us when I see the first spark. It is just a glimmer really, something seen out of the corner of my eye. Then I notice some more.

"It's coming," Tam says.

"Quickly," Palina orders. "We must get to the cave. Hurry, Alex."

I'm moving as fast as I can, but I'm also checking out the clouds. It's a regular light show, with small, jagged sparks of lightning leaping from cloud to cloud. It doesn't look particularly dangerous—the clouds are a hundred feet or so above us. Except for one thing. The bolts seem to be growing. With each leap from cloud to cloud, they grow brighter and brighter, their flashes illuminating this side of the mountain.

We are crawling into the cave, small and cold, when I get my first look at Living Lightning.

At first it appears to be nothing more than a big sphere of lightning careening into the mountain and bouncing off. But then it takes form until standing in front of us is some kind of creature completely composed of lightning. It has two jagged legs, pincer arms, and a head that zigzags its way to a point. There are no eyes. But there is a sort of hole that keeps opening and closing, while the pointy head tilts back and forth.

Palina is pulling Tam into the cave and the safety of gravity. The creature starts to curl up and lunge.

Right in my direction.

Roll 3 D6.

If the total is less than or equal to Alex's value for Intelligence, turn to section 57.

If the total is greater than Alex's value for Intelligence, decide what Alex will do.

If he tries to dodge the Lightning creature, turn to section 67.

If he draws a sword, turn to section 60.

* **73** *

One of the knights brings his flying horse up toward the left. I have it in my sight, really have it, and I fire.

Another miss.

But he isn't gunning for me. The bastard has Palina picked out.

And she doesn't even see him.

"Palina!" I yell.

He fires, and I hear her scream.

I throw my gun to the ground.

"Wait!" I yell as another knight comes bearing down toward us.

"She's hurt, I've got to—"

The voice that answers me is metallic, like the suit he wears.

"You surrender, varlet?"

Tam has already crawled to her sister. "Yes. Now, can I help her?"

The knight gets off his horse, which stays there floating while it whirrs and whines. He pulls out a sword.

"Put them in chains."

Another knight arrives with chains that look like they are more than adequate to hold King Kong.

"How is she?" I ask Tam.

"It's a nasty wound," Tam says. "I can't stop the bleeding from her shoulder. I'll need something from the pack."

Turn to section 87.

* **74** *

The lightning creature crackles into the rock, sending watery drops of electricity trickling down the mountainside.

I don't really stop and watch the splendor of it all. I'm too busy scrambling as fast as I can into the cave while Palina reaches out and pulls me in.

Not much gravity, I notice, as I pop up a bit too quickly and bang my head into the cave ceiling.

There's no time for nursing my bump as the lightning creature steps into the cave.

"What's its problem?" I ask Palina.

"Territoriality," she says. "This is their world."

Its jagged, pointy head twitches left and right as if deciding which one of us to confront. The cave is small, made even more unpleasant by a thick layer of ice surrounding the walls.

"So how do we stop it?"

Palina pauses. "I don't know."

"Great," I mutter. Then I see its head pointing in my direction. It has obviously decided whom it wants.

Roll 3 D6.

If the total is less than or equal to Alex's value for Wisdom, turn to section 59.

If the total is greater than Alex's value for Wisdom, turn to section 71.

* **75** *

The bridge is just ahead, spanning the murky, silty river that curves lazily around the nearby hills. It's a simple wooden bridge.

"Over that hill," Tam says, "should be the town."

"If we're there by nightfall, we may be able to start tonight," Palina says to me.

"Start what, princess? Can you fill me in?"

"Let's just get there, Alex. The plan will sit better with a bit of dinner."

"Dinner! Anything but these meals of fruits and nuts," Tam yells, running across the bridge. "I'm sick of them."

Her voice, light and carefree, echoes back to us and we run to catch up with her.

"Me too," a voice booms out. We freeze in our tracks. Then a great bear of a man stomps out from behind a tree. "Neatly done," he says, pointing in the direction of the river.

"Rufo!" Tam and Palina say together, running over to him.

They throw their arms around him. This Rufo is big, solid, and wearing a healthy sword that looks like it has been well used.

"This is Rufo," Palina says. Then, more quietly, "He's our most loyal friend."

"My aunt speaks too kindly," he says.

"Aunt?" I say, noticing that Palina has to be a good thirty years younger than Rufo.

"My grandmother is the empress," he says proudly. "The old lady of course went on making kids long after I was born."

"Whatever you say," chalking up the confusing genealogy to my lack of experience in this odd world.

"Why are you here?" Palina asks quickly.

Rufo encircles all of us with his arms, and pulls us tightly.

"Because," he says, "there's been a small change in plans."

Turn to section 93.

* **76** *

"They seemed genuinely scared when I said where we were going. So let's follow them."

Palina turns to Tam. "Tam, are you sensing anything?"

Tam closes her eyes, and I hear her breathing change. "No, nothing at all. I'm sorry . . ."

"Hey, not to worry, sprout." I turn back to the leader of the flying dwarves. "Okay, lead on."

One by one they turn and bank to the left, and we follow them. It's anything but a quiet hike through the woods. At first, all we have to deal with is the noise level, the little guys chattering with each other in high-pitched voices that remind me of a Chip'n'Dale cartoon. But then I get hit in the head with some kind of nut.

"Ouch," I call out. I assume that it has fallen from a tree, but then when I resume walking, another one plops down . . . and another. And it seems to me that the Mischief Men are always looking some other way when I get bopped.

"Whoever's throwing nuts at me can stop now. Joke's over."

And the forest explodes into laughter. That's just the first joke. Later, the Mischief Men begin scrambling backward, eyes wide open, like they've just seen Godzilla. There is, of course, nothing there. They just want to give us a fright. And when I go off to the side of the woods to relieve myself, all the Mischief Men follow, finding me in midstream, pointing and whispering what I think must be rude comments.

Tam gets a purple worm stuck down her back. ("It likes you," one of the Mischief Men tries to explain, exploding into giggles, "it really likes you.")

And Palina is distracted as she crosses a small stream, and two of the Mischief Men trip her.

"All right," she yells. "Enough is enough. I don't know what you think that you are up to, but we are not here to play jokes."

Of course, they all scatter when she yells, but one of the Mischief Men comes back and tries to explain.

"It's how we live," he says apologetically, almost sadly. "We always trick each other. It's as natural to us as breathing is to you. And just as necessary."

Palina looks at him. His cohorts are all hovering and hiding, sad-eyed, behind the large trees. "That's all well and good," she says sternly, "but we've had enough tricks for today. Is it much farther to the river?"

He seems to brighten. "No, not at all. In fact," he says, performing a loop-de-loop, "it's right through there." The Mischief Man points to an opening in the woods.

We forget their pranks and march briskly to the river. Tam has one of the smallish Mischief Men sitting on her shoulder, chatting. After a few minutes we arrive at the river.

It's big, a broad, salty river that flows gently.

"We must leave you now. This is as far as we go. Thanks," the leader announces, "for letting us play with you."

"But wait," I say. "How can we get across?"

"Try flying," he suggests, and then he and the other Mischief Men are gone.

I turn to Palina. "Any ideas?"

"Swim. Tam's backpack is waterproof."

It's a good distance to the other side. I don't know how good a swimmer Tam is.

"Perhaps it's not deep," Tam says. "We might just be able to walk across."

"We don't seem to have any choice," Palina says. "Tam, make sure everything is closed tightly and give the pack to Alex. I'll go first. We'll walk as far as we can, then swim. The town is just the other side of that hill. We're almost there . . ."

For a moment, I think I see Palina and Tam give each other a secret look.

But I try not to give in to my paranoia.

Turn to section 66.

* **77** *

Maybe it's because I don't trust myself with a gun. A couple of misses, and the overgrown eel will dive under the water, back to its slimy burrow, with Palina for lunch.

Or maybe I feel more comfortable with a sword, more able to kill the ugly thing.

I rush to it and pull back to take a swing.

It blinks at me, giving me an impressive display of its teeth.

EEL
To hit Alex: 12   To be hit: 10   Hit points: 10
Damage: 1 D6+1   Damage with sword: 1 D6

Alex attacks first. If he hits it, the eel will drop Palina and retreat. Turn to section 80.

If Alex misses, and the eel hits, turn to section 81.

* **78** *

I see the beam of light go whizzing right past the creature. Then the eel rears up and seems ready to dive under the water.

"Aim lower!" Tam yells. "You went too high!"

"Right," I whisper, and I press the button again.

To hit the eel: 10
Roll 3 D6.

If Alex hits the eel, turn to section 80.

If Alex misses the eel, turn to section 81.

* **79** *

I bring the unwieldy gun up quickly, and the eel seems to catch a glimpse of me. (At any rate, it opens its mouth, displaying nicely curved rows of jagged teeth.)

My thumb feels the trigger stud, and I look through the sight. At any moment the creature might dive under the water.

Gently, I push the button.

To hit the eel: 10
Roll 3 D6.

If the total is less than or equal to 10, turn to section 80.

If the total is greater than 10, turn to section 78.

* 80 *

I hit the eel, and even I can't believe my good fortune. It loosens its body, and Palina plops into the water. Then it dives away, disappearing into the muck.

I race to her . . . she is floating lifelessly on the water.

"She's alive," Tam says.

"What?" I say, pulling her out of the water. "How do you—oh, yeah, I keep forgetting."

"But she's hurt. Bring her to the shore," Tam orders.

"I wasn't about to stop here, Tam."

I trudge through the water, holding Palina beside me, and then I carry her out.

I lay her on the shore.

"Give her some of this." Tam hands me a canteen filled with a dark red liquid. I gently lower it toward Palina's lips. Palina tastes it, and then her mouth opens, eagerly sucking at it.

"It will warm her, give her some strength," Tam explains.

"I'm alive?" Palina asks, blinking awake.

"I think so, princess. Either that or we're all ghosts. Shall we camp here for the night?"

Section 80

She shakes her head. "No. Let me rest a bit. But we must get to the city tonight."

"I don't think—"

"Tonight," she orders.

"That's a good idea," a voice booms out.

"Rufo!" Tam and Palina say together, running over to him.

They throw their arms around him. This Rufo is big, solid, and wearing a healthy sword that looks like it has been well used.

"This is Rufo," Palina says. Then, more quietly, "He's our most loyal friend."

"My aunt speaks too kindly," he says.

"Aunt?" I say, noticing that Palina has to be a good thirty years younger than Rufo.

"My grandmother is the empress," he says proudly. "The old lady of course went on making kids long after I was born."

"Whatever you say," chalking up the confusing genealogy to my lack of experience in this odd world.

"Why are you here?" Palina asks quickly.

Rufo encircles all of us with his arms, and pulls us tightly.

"Because," he says, "there's been a small change in plans."

Turn to section 93.

* **81** *

The eel dives into the mucky river and then—surprise—it surfaces right next to me.

Palina has been released from its coiled body. It only has eyes for me now, and with vicious speed it closes its mouth over my upper torso—

(And believe me, the stench is incredible!)—and bites down . . .

Turn to section 29.

* **82** *

Why are all of Willy's guards constructs? The only humans that I have seen so far are his two agents from the marketplace.

Can it be that old King William isn't all that well liked? If that's the case, I may have more help later on than I know about.

Turn to section 92.

* **83** *

Somehow, my easy patter doesn't sound quite right in William's throne room. I think that the kerchief trick might be a good effect, but they look bored when I throw it into the air and it changes color.

When I toss it again, returning it to rainbow hues, he snaps his fingers and it stops in midair.

"Scan," he says, and I hear some electronic sensors whining.

He looks at the small screen he holds in his lap. "Aha, of course, that's how it's done. Not so impressive, magician."

Right, I think. Not when you can perform an autopsy on my magical apparatus.

"For my next trick," I continue casually, wondering if I'm laying the biggest egg in my career, "perhaps some card play might interest your majesty."

He seems more interested in the maid, who has returned with another goblet of wine. If I'm not wrong, he's starting to slosh his Rs around.

I hold the deck out in front of him, face

down. "Pick a card, your majesty." He reaches out, his slender hand almost serpentine. He glances at the card and grins. "Now please replace it in the deck and I will tell you what card you selected."

This trick the boy seems to like.

"It's an ace of spades," he says.

I look at him dumbfounded. "But I'm supposed to tell *you* what card you picked."

"But I," he says, smiling triumphantly, "told you first."

"But you knew what it was . . . you looked at it," I say in exasperation, trying to explain to him just how he derailed the trick.

"Sore loser," he says, and I think I see him give one of the knights a small wave of his hand.

(Am I about to get the hook? I wonder.)

"Let me prepare my next illusion, your highness, the disappearing wand . . ."

Tam is next to me, helping me prepare the table for the trick. A knight starts down the escalator (about as incongruous a sight as I've seen since leaving sunny Florida). Tam is breathing heavily, as if she were having trouble catching her breath.

"Someone's hurt," she says.

"Hurt?" I ask, smiling at William as I speak sotto voce. "Who? Rufo, Palina . . . ?"

"I . . . I can't tell. They're still coming . . . almost here, but," and she looks at me. "I don't think we'll have enough time."

As if to accentuate Tam's point, William slides off his massive bed.

"Very nice," he says. "Very nice, indeed. But I'm afraid that we are just about out of time, magician. Now, if you'll just pack up your magic set, we'll see about . . . rewarding you for your services to the crown."

"We need more time," Tam says. "Alex, you've got to give us time."

"Right, sprout, right. Don't you worry about it."

I walk over to William. "But, sire, you've not seen my greatest illusion, one that no magician before me has ever attempted."

He stares right at me, his eyes narrow, snakelike.

Roll 3 D6.

If the total is less than or equal to Alex's value for Charisma, turn to section 94.

If the total is greater than Alex's value for Charisma, turn to section 91.

* **84** *

I start performing the trick, my last trick, almost normally.

But as I get close to the point where I'll reach into the bottom of the magic chest and pull out the ray gun, I become increasingly more fidgety.

And good old Bad William seems to notice.

He arches his eyebrows, squints, and otherwise makes his esthetically displeasing face even more so.

Move it, man, I say to myself.

I pull out the ray gun.

"Surprise," I whisper, unable to resist a bit of magical chutzpah. Bad William wastes no time in reacting. He looks right and left at his guards, and they begin plodding forward, unsheathing their swords.

I try to fire, but nothing happens.

"He's doing something," I hiss to Tam. "I can't—"

"I know . . ." she says, her face grim (and if there's anything inappropriate in this world, it's a grim eleven-year-old).

Whatever she's trying to do has the desired effect on Bad William.

"Now!" she yells. "Fire."
I press down on the button.

Alex will get three chances to fire before the knights arrive.
He must roll 10 or less on 3 D6 to hit.

If he hits William, turn to section 99.

If he has not hit William by the end of the second round, turn to section 97.

* **85** *

We climb a small hill, just past the river, and see the grotesque splendor of Bad William's town. Obviously constructed out of the fantasies of his demented mind. It is beautiful, and it is grotesque; it looks like King Arthur meets Vegas.

I think immediately of Neuschwanstein, Mad King Ludwig of Bavaria's storybook castle that he built in the nineteenth century. He created the ideal setting to invite his pal, composer Richard Wagner, to come and give exclusive performances of his overtures for a royal audience of one. But the splendid castle, perched on a mountaintop, nearly bankrupted the Bavarian treasury, and Ludwig later died mysteriously.

A hundred years later, Walt Disney modeled his Disneyland palace on crazy Ludwig's fun house.

But this puts both of them to shame.

I can see workers still struggling to finish part of the great walled city and the castle. It has dozens of peaked roofs and enough widow's walks to accommodate a corps of be-

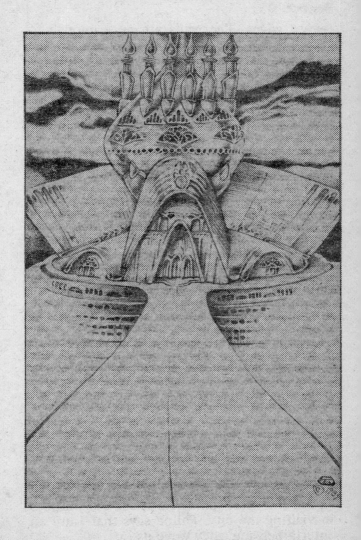

reaved wives. The walls are huge enough to stop a giant, and an enormous field fills the right part of town, festooned with hundreds of flags.

(I later learn that games, of a most vicious and demented sort, go on all the time there—night and day. Just in case the "king" should desire to make an appearance.)

But perhaps the strangest touch of all is the enormous electrical sign that stretches across nearly the entire front wall. It is turned off now, since the sun has still another few hours of light, but at night I'm sure it's visible from miles away.

It's like one of those placards people place outside their suburban homes, "The Smiths." Only this sign is the size of the Chrysler Building.

And all it says is "William."

"I think he might be overcompensating."

"What do you mean?" Rufo asks, turning to me.

"Nothing. What do we do now?"

"Tam, can you sense anything?"

She shakes her head.

"Very well, then, let's go inside the city."

Rufo comes over and slaps my back. "It's almost show time, Alex."

We enter the city easily, joining hordes of other visitors also walking around like bumpkin tourists, gaping at Bad William's creation. At the entrance, some guards ask our purpose in visiting the city. Palina says that I am an entertainer, and they wave us in.

Once inside, guards are everywhere, dressed in a strange mixture of Roman legionnaire, medieval knight, and McDonald Land employee. William's tastes are obviously eclectic, and he has no concern for clashing styles, color schemes, or architecture.

Palina stops one guard, and batting her baby blues, she asks directions to the city square.

We pass shops selling goods from all over the universes.

"Look," Tam yells excitedly, "Nevian wine!"

Palina spots boutiques featuring the latest fashions from Center (some of which include intriguing dresses that leave little to the imagination).

"I'd like to see you in one of those," I say quietly to Palina.

"I have a whole closetful back on Center," she replies. "Let us get through this, and I'll wear one to the celebration party."

Rufo stops at a gun shop and eyes some small, hand-held ray guns.

There are also slaves. I notice dour-faced city dwellers obviously tending to the needs of some of William's more favored citizens.

"They're wearing control bracelets," Palina says. "If they tried to escape, they'd die. They're slaves for life."

"And there hasn't been slavery in the Twenty Universes for over four thousand years," Rufo says with disgust.

I start hearing the sounds of the marketplace well before we can see anything. It's the roar of a huge, milling crowd, much like that at a circus or some convention.

"Stay close to me, Tam," Rufo says.

Then we turn down a street, and the great city courtyard lies before us, over a square mile offering everything from four-armed leprechaunlike tap dancers performing on a makeshift stage to a pushcart selling the same type of shish kebab you can get on Sixth Avenue and 42nd Street.

The sun goes down, and I'm momentarily startled to see three moons appear in the sky.

"Wait here," Palina orders as she walks over to a chunky fellow dressed in an official-looking orange tunic. He has a big "W" embroidered on his lapel. Money changes hands, and Palina returns.

"I've got a stall near here. As soon as we get there I want you to start your performance. Be loud, noisy, get people's attention—Bad William's spies will eventually come by."

The stall is sandwiched between a rumor-monger (you pay him some money and he tells you the latest dirt) and someone offering a Nevian specialty—froglike animals in bowls of ice.

"Yum," Tam says, poking me. "See what's next to us?"

"You like that stuff? You know, you're one crazy kid. How you could—"

Rufo walks over to the frog salesman, plops down a coin, and pops one in his mouth. I wait for him to let out a satisfied belch.

But Palina tells me to get started. Tam pulls

the magic set out of her pack (which I now believe could hold a Volkswagen) and they open it up.

"You're on," Palina says.

"Right." The set comes with its own portable table, but the stall also has a platform. I spread my stuff out and launch into my routine.

"Ladies and gentlemen, boys and girls, prepare yourselves to be mystified and amazed. I, Alex the Magnificent, have traveled a great distance—too great actually—to bring you deep magic from another world."

Most of the crowd keeps on passing me, inured to pitches. I mean, competition here is tough. Of course, in the alleyway is a tattooed belly dancer whose stomach can change pictures. She's currently telling a story—on her belly—of one of the more steamy thousand and one nights. Even I wouldn't have minded checking out her act.

But I have a show to do.

Turn to section 90.

* **86** *

Naturally enough, I fumble the stupid gun getting it out of the chest. I can pull rabbits out of hats and I can slice people in two, but can I simply bring the gun up to eye level and shoot?

No way. It slips out of my nervous hands and goes tumbling to the floor.

William notices my fidgeting and glances at me, reaching for the gun just as it leaps out of my fingers.

He sneers, making his already ugly mug even less esthetically pleasing. Then Tam is there, catching the gun like a wide receiver. Without missing a beat she hands me the gun and says, "He's given the guards orders to attack!"

And sure enough, the guards are stepping forward, sliding their behemoth swords out of their scabbards, ready to play slice and dice with me and Tam.

I try to aim the gun.

But William, whose sneer has now transformed into a supercilious gloating expression, has his fingers up before him and I know that the gun won't work.

"He's stopped me, Tam . . . can you do something?"

Tam's face looks far too serious for an eleven-year-old. "I'll try, Alex. But this is his world, his 'magic.'" She screws up her face, and I see something register in Bad William. I feel a glimmer of hope.

If only the guards weren't about ten feet away and slicing the air like windmills.

I squint (cinematic thoughts of *High Noon* and *Back to Bataan* running through my mind) and blast away.

For Alex to hit William, he must roll 10 or less on 3 D6.

If he hits, turn to section 99.

After the first round, the first knight is in striking distance.
To hit Alex: 8   Damage: 1 D6+1
After the knight attacks, Alex can fire again, followed by the arrival of another knight, etc.

If Alex hits William this time, turn to section 99.

If Alex has no hit points left, turn to section 29.

After Alex's third shot, turn to section 97.

* **87** *

"Rufo," Tam squeals.

The remaining knights turn, but are soon vaporized under the careful ministrations of this Rufo character. He's a great bear of a man, dressed in a mixture of skins and furs. He has a heavy orangish beard that fits his oversize skull. He comes over to us laughing, but keeps his gun raised, wary of more attackers.

"You looked like you needed some help."

He sees the wounds we have taken then, and with the calm air of a professional, he proceeds to bandage them. He uncorks some deep red liquid and insists that we all drink.

"It will get you back on your feet," he orders. "Oh," he says, handing the flask to me, "we haven't been properly introduced, now have we? I'm Oscar's First Lieutenant, and I'm Tam and Palina's nephew."

"Nephew!"

"Yes, but don't trouble yourself figuring out genealogy here. Long-life treatments have everything all mixed up. The old lady—"

"He means the empress, his grandmother," Palina says reprovingly.

"She likes to look and act young," Rufo says.

"Why are you here?" Palina asks.

"Let's just say," Rufo replies with a broad grin, "that Oscar had a change of heart." He looks right at me. "There's been a change of plans, lad."

Turn to section 93.

* **88** *

Somehow that old show time magic just isn't there. I mean, I've performed for everything from kids in diapers to Old Folk luncheons. And I've always had some fun with it.

But doing my act for this demented idiot is bringing no pleasure at all.

I just hope that I can keep him amused until Rufo and Palina arrive.

Roll 3 D6

If the total is less than or equal to Alex's value for Wisdom, turn to section 96.

If the total is greater than Alex's value for Wisdom, turn to section 89.

∗ **89** ∗

What would most impress this degenerate, I wonder, and what would bore him? Is card magic too sedate, or will he have trouble relating to the disappearing rabbit trick?

I don't have a clue.

After all, he isn't the typical fun-loving audience.

Turn to section 83.

* **90** *

I start out small. (I mean, there isn't any crowd yet except for one dull-eyed bumpkin standing out front. And he seems to be more interested in looking at Palina.)

"Why, yes, I have brought incredible illusions from the four corners of the globe to entertain you good people of Ba—I mean—King William's fair city."

My lone customer is so close to the magic table that it seems likely I'll bop him on the nose while performing.

"Would you mind stepping back, sir. Other people would like to see . . ."

I pull a rainbow-colored handkerchief out of my case. "So many colors," I say dramatically. "So many . . ." I flip it into the air and it changes to a bright red.

The bumpkin claps (so easily entertained) and then the seed of a crowd begins to form. I catch the kerchief, wave it in the air, and it changes colors again.

I move along to something a tad more sophisticated. "My young assistant here," I gesture for Tam to come closer, "will help me in my next illusion. Observe this length of rope."

The rope trick has to be one of the most basic, yet effective, of magic tricks. Nimble fingers are the key. The rope is looped in one's hand so that it looks like it is being cut into small pieces. But actually, only very small, almost unnoticeable links are severed (and quickly discarded).

"They don't have any stage magicians on this world?" I mumble to Tam. "I can't believe it."

"There's no call for it." She pops a bubble, and I make a mental note to remind her that there should be no gum if we get into the castle. A king is still a king, even if he's a bad one. "You see, Alex, magic is like a science in most of the universes. It's something you can actually do. But what you do appears impossible."

Rufo sidles up to me, a big grin on his face. But his eyes tell me that he is in no joking mood. "Good work, my boy. The crowd is growing. Soon you'll get the attention of William's agents."

The audience cheers when the cut string is shown to be—ta-da!—in one piece.

"You've got to show me how you do that," Tam says.

"Sure, just as soon as . . ."

Then I see them. They're dressed in red, one tall, the other short and squat. They wear pointy caps with gold "W"s embroidered on them. The costumes look like they were lifted from the fun days of the Spanish Inquisition. And their ugly grey faces tell me that they would have been perfectly at home during the rollicking days of boiling oil and screaming recantations. Palina strolls down to point out the obvious.

"To your left," she whispers.

"I've got eyes." I feel inside my case for my next trick. For a moment I can't feel it, and I think one of my best tricks will have to go unperformed. Then I feel the equipment.

"Now, ladies and gentlemen, the Strange Case of the Disappearing Rabbit."

I hear the crowd buzzing . . .

"What's wrong?" I ask out of the side of my mouth to Tam.

"They don't know what rabbits are."

Not skipping a beat, I pick up one of the larger foam animals. "Yes, folks, this a rabbit, a cute, furry little animal. They love carrots. Now, we shall make it multiply and then disappear."

The dour-faced representatives of William pull closer, and the crowd wastes no time clearing a path for them. If nothing else, those two jokers have clout.

I make the rabbit disappear from some yokel's hand. (He proceeds to look up his own sleeve, and then on the ground, while the crowd laughs at him. They'd probably enjoy a good bear-baiting.)

"They're probing," Tam whispers. She

means that the two red-robed hoods have some psychic ability and they are checking out my vitae.

"Can you block it?" I ask, my smile plastered on my face.

"I think so." She pops a pink bubble. "It's not too powerful."

"And you, sir," I say, abruptly grabbing the taller of the two agents. "Do you think you're carrying any rabbits with you?"

His eyes narrow.

"Surely *you* don't have any rabbits." A small grin crosses his face. Everybody loves to perform. Put anyone on a stage, and they turn into a giggly school kid.

"No, I'm sure that—"

And I lift off his hood.

(The crowd gasps when I do that—apparently it's a no-no.)

But when they see a whole family of foam rabbits pop off his balding dome, the crowd breaks into applause, and even he smiles.

I see the other one speaking into something, then he pulls his buddy back. I start my next trick.

The short, stubby one comes over to me.

"Excuse me, but King William would very much like to study your talents up close."

"Certainly," I say. "Just as soon as I'm finished with this performance—"

"I'm afraid it'll have to be now," the short one says, and from out of nowhere guards appear to escort the crowd away.

Rufo is at my ear. "The gun and sword are hidden in the bottom of your case. But insist on Tam going with you."

At first, they balk at my bringing Tam. But I explain that I simply can't perform without her. Reluctantly, they agree.

"The King is at the games," they explain, waiting for me to pack and shut my case. "You'll meet him there and proceed to the palace."

Rufo and Palina watch us walk away, and I give them my best thumbs-up smile and wave.

Tam seems nervous, chewing her gum more ferociously now. A lot depends upon her, and she's just a kid.

Then again, a lot depends on me.

And I'm just a stage magician.

If ever there was a time to heroically rise to the challenge, I guess now is it.

Turn to section 95.

* **91** *

"Enough, magician, I've seen enough of your twaddle. Your foolishness holds little interest. Of course, I'll study your equipment later, at my leisure. But now," he laughs hollowly, "the show is over."

"When is the train due, Tam?" I whisper.

"I . . . I'm not sure. There's been a problem."

William is slinking over to one of his guards, a mindless golem who I feel can dispatch me and Tam with ease.

"I guess, sprout, we're out of time."

I dig into the chest, push a latch opening a secret compartment, and dig out the compact ray gun. "Here goes nothing," I mutter.

Turn to section 86.

* 92 *

"Ha! Good one!" he squeals. "Go for an-other!"

He's looking to stage right of the arena. (There are easily three or four football-size fields, each offering, or preparing to offer, a different game.)

The "games" William is watching are sick.

A knight (probably a construct) chases an unarmed human with a jousting lance. Both of them are on flying, mechanical horses that have incredible maneuverability. But like a cat cornering a mouse, it seems like only a matter of time before the human will be skewered.

The one William is watching already has a good chunk out of his leg, and the construct is bearing down.

Now I know William's problem.

He's a psychopath.

One of the red men goes up to William's ear and whispers something, probably announcing my appearance.

"Soon, soon," he squeals petulantly. "This one's almost gone." He scoops up some red and yellow items from a bowl—they look like ju-jubes. Later, I learn they are the frozen larval form of some uncommonly sweet insect.

And sure enough, the human is soon skewered. (I can't look. But the roar of the crowd tells me that some major violence has just taken place. Some things just don't change, no matter what universe you're in.)

Then William spins around, chuckling, his legs draped over the arm rest, to face Tam and me.

"A magician, eh?"

I nod.

"'Yes, sire,' is how we answer around here."

"Yes, sire."

He pauses, as if weighing the sincerity of my answer. He is thin, almost gaunt. Whatever his vices, eating isn't one of them. But the wild look in his eyes indicates that he might have a penchant for ingesting psychoactive substances.

This guy is obviously totally out of control.

"And this must be your apprentice, eh, magician?"

I don't like his eyes on Tam. He is a foul, despicable creature, and it suddenly seems very wrong to have her here.

"My assistant . . . I can't do some of the tricks without her."

He arches his eyebrows at me, catching onto my fear that he might be viewing Tam as dispensable. "Why, then, you shall have her. You see, magician," he says, standing up and walking close to me, "I like magic. I've learned tricks that even that old bitch the empress doesn't know. Unfortunately," he laughs eerily, "most of them are extremely nasty." He raises a hand, and even a few feet away from him, I can feel heat radiating from it.

"My face," the tall agent suddenly groans. "Not my face, sire."

"Just a small demonstration, counselor. Nothing too drastic."

My hands go slowly over Tam's eyes, covering them. The man's face grows bright red, and then tiny bubbles, small heat blisters, begin to appear. He screams (and Tam clutches me).

"No more, sire, I beg you."

Another, larger blister forms and pops on one cheek.

"I get the idea." But William seems entranced by his human marshmallow.

"Sire," the chubby one says, "they're starting archery."

"Oh, archery," he grins. "*That* is one of my favorites."

The field has filled with people with bull's-eyes painted on them. They scurry back and forth while archers—more constructs, I guess—shoot arrows at them.

Now I know why they call him Bad William in the twenty other universes.

"I am ready to perform, if your majesty would like to see."

He watches a few of the targets fall and then turns to me.

"Yes, perhaps you can show me a new trick or two. Come, counselor," he says to the chubby one, "bring the magician to my chambers. And his young friend." Nobody helps the other "counselor," whose painful whimpering is drowned out by the bloodthirsty roar of the circuslike crowd.

William leads the way, followed by his constructs and then, finally, the counselor, Tam, and me.

"Are they following?" I whisper to Tam, wondering about Palina and Rufo.

"Yes," she says with some hesitation. "I think so. I lost contact, before, when—"

"I know. Right when William was showing off, the bastard." And right now, I undergo a change.

Before, I was here pretty much because I had to be (only if because I wanted to get home). But now I have another, more lofty, goal. I want to rid this corrupted world of its King William.

I have crossed the line from unwilling accomplice to the empress's hero. It's funny the tricks life can play on you.

The route to William's castle is anything but direct. Hidden passageways lead to stairs, which in turn lead to elevators, before we finally arrive at an enormous escalator that seemed lifted from Macy's.

Tam is, I hope, keeping an eye on the route and beaming the info to her sister.

Me, I'm checking out the artwork.

Bad William must have the greatest collection of bad art in the universe. There's a whole gallery devoted to felt paintings, including depictions of both the fifties and Vegas Elvis, as well as scenes of undraped women posing in all their muscular wonder.

(How come I never meet anyone like that?)

One wall is filled with "original oils" of big-eyed children holding flowers and puppies, revealing William's sloppy, sentimental side.

Some of the other art, though, massive holograms of gruesome alien creatures ripping each other apart, is even harder to stomach. I'm sure that such a demented fellow as William must have a "private" collection of art that would make even the fun guys of the Third Reich blink.

The escalator leads, not to handbags and household furnishings, but to William's personal chambers. Here we come into a world of hotel glitz run amok. A bed the size of a handball court, a bubbling stream next to it (unless it was a pot for cooking unwanted counselors), three-dimensional tapestries on the walls featuring the heroic exploits of William, and everywhere knights standing guard.

I look back at the escalator. If Rufo and Palina attempt to come up that way, they'll be dead before they reach the halfway mark.

"Tam," I whisper, checking our host to see if he is listening. William slips out of one cloak and changes into something more casual. A French maid appears, complete with high heels and black mini-dress, holding a tray with a huge goblet, which William takes quickly. "Tam, can you pick up any other way in here?"

Section 92

Her face is screwed up. She is struggling, and has been for a long time now. Not only is she blocking my thoughts so that William just takes me to be a talented performer, but she is also sending difficult instructions to her sister.

Maybe, I think grimly, it's too much for her.

"I'm trying," she says quickly, "but I can't see anything, only—"

"Magician," William announces, plopping down on the bed (and I just bet it has magic fingers), "I'm ready for my show. I have sensors that will, if you don't mind, make a holographic record of everything you do, so I can . . . study it later," he smiles. "At my leisure. Don't worry, though. You'll be well rewarded."

I smile back at him. Right, I'm sure I'll be well rewarded, maybe I'll get to play joust or archery. Won't that be fun?

He takes a deep sip from his goblet, and his face grows more solemn.

"You may begin."

Turn to section 88.

* 93 *

We walk and listen to Rufo. "The original plan called for you and Tam to enter William's castle. The fool's a sucker for magic, Alex. Any trick he doesn't know, he wants to make his own. Fortunately, he doesn't know enough about Earth to understand that all you do is sleight of hand."

I bristle a bit at his denigration of my art, but Rufo takes no notice.

"Tam was to protect you from mental probes by William's counselors while you perform. At the opportune moment, you were to whip a cutlass or a death ray out of your bag of tricks. Tam would be long gone by then, and the odds were, my boy, that you wouldn't escape alive."

Palina turns away—the secret agenda of our little trip is finally out.

"But we've reconsidered. It was too dangerous to Tam, and Palina, and," he laughs, "certainly for you."

Rufo is a big man, but he carries himself effortlessly. He's just the kind of guy I'd want in a fight—as long as he was on my side. "And now?"

Section 93

"Now, Tam will still go in with you—your stage assistant—but she'll be sending instructions to her sister, and we'll follow. You'll still get the honor of removing Bad William. But we'll see that his guards don't stop you. You may even get out of this alive, my boy."

"That would be nice."

"Ah," Rufo says. "There it is." And Rufo stops, his arms draped around Palina and Tam. "The wonderful city of Bad William."

Turn to section 85.

* **94** *

I had him; he was hooked and had to see the trick.

"Very well," he says, his eyes opening wide again. "Let me see this miracle. But first, I would like a refill."

He hoists up his goblet in the air while I busy myself about my table.

I've just bought an extra few minutes . . . but is it enough?

"Soon, Tam?" I ask.

She looks at me, smiles weakly, and answers, "Any minute now, Alex . . . any minute."

Turn to section 84.

∗ **95** ∗

The two guys who look like Red Lobster waiters don't have much to say as they lead us through the maze of Bad William's town. And for a planned community, this is the pits. There just doesn't seem to be one decent thoroughfare that runs the length of the city. Paris, with its quaint and confusing *rues* to nowhere, and Venice's alleyways that turn into canals are both a piece of cake to navigate compared to this burg.

The guy with the street map concession must be raking in the dough.

Eventually, we come to the walled area that encloses the playing fields.

"You getting all these twists and turns down, Tam?"

She nods. "It's the palace I'm worried about. If it's anything like this mess, I'm going to have a tough time giving Palina instructions."

We've been whispering, even though our guides are well ahead of us, but soon the raucous sound of bells, whistles, and screaming reaches our ears.

I half expected to see beer-bellied buffoons wearing Jets sweatshirts and beanies having tailgate parties.

It's the main entrance to the arena, blocked by hundreds of people trying to get in.

"What's wrong?" I shout up to William's lackeys.

"It's full," the chubby one answers. "They are waiting for seats to become free."

"Must be some show."

"Oh, it most certainly is," he says. "We will be going in by the side door, leading directly to King William's review stand."

"Box seats," I say sarcastically.

I notice that the people we pass give Tweedledum and Dee a wide berth. Maybe I shouldn't be treating them so cavalierly.

They approach a door—more of a metal gate, really—guarded by two knights that tower over eight feet each.

"Constructs," Tam whispers.

They have the great metal door ready and open as we arrive. We saunter past them and I pick up the distant aroma of what smells like sausage. I almost ask Tam about the overpowering smell, but I decide that I'd rather not know just where it comes from.

More guards—standing stock-still—litter a curved staircase that spirals its way to the very top of the arena. A whole gaggle of constructs greets us at the top, lining the way to Bad William's season seat.

Section 95

Roll 3 D6.

If the total is less than or equal to Alex's value for Intelligence, turn to section 82.

If the total is greater than Alex's value for Intelligence, turn to section 92.

* **96** *

As long as I can hold his interest, the more time I can give Palina to arrive.

Pacing, in a magic act, is everything. It's important to mix some close-up work with big stage effects.

I think carefully about the order of tricks, and then, arranging my magic table in front of William's obscenely large bed, I begin.

Add +1 to Alex's Dexterity and Charisma values while he's performing for William.

Then turn to section 83.

* **97** *

"Well, it looks like we arrived not a moment too soon, eh, Alex?"

I make a slight turn to see who is talking in such a booming voice, and am more than overjoyed to see—

"Rufo! Palina!" Tam screams out.

But Rufo is wasting no time on pleasantries.

He takes his sword (I wonder why he didn't simply fire his gun) and starts chopping William's construct-knights into little pieces.

"Hurry up, Alex," Palina says, "we can't hold them off forever." Palina is relying on her gun to keep the knights at bay.

(And I think—why doesn't she take a pot shot at William? Surely her aim is better than mine.)

Tam picks up on my thoughts.

"Because you're the hero, Alex. You're the one who'll become the legend on this world. It's your job to stop William."

Right, I think. I'm the hero. About as unlikely a role for me as I can imagine, but there you have it. Alex Tanen—prestidigitator, illusionist, and savior of worlds.

Once again I sight the crazy bastard in my

gun. Tam groans, beginning to weaken in her psychic battle with William.

I press the trigger.

Nice and steady.

After all, I'm the hero.

For Alex to hit Bad William, roll 3 D6.

If the total is less than or equal to 10, turn to section 99.

If he misses, turn to section 102.

* **98** *

Well, look at it this way, I tell myself. What's there for me on Earth? More one-night stands in the Poconos and small-town Kiwanis meetings. Besides, I don't particularly like performing. I like magic, the art of illusion.

And the million dollars? All the money on Earth couldn't create a world as sublimely beautiful as this.

I look at Oscar (and try to give a quick glance at Palina). Tam is next to her, and they both watch me as if they know something is up.

"Okay, I've decided, Easy Gordon."

If Alex decides to stay, turn to section 100.

If Alex returns to Earth, turn to section 103.

* 99 *

The ray gun is an interesting weapon. It emits a thin beam of light, bright and intense, but otherwise looks harmless. The target, if hit, seems to develop a slowly growing hole that radiates outward. In a moment, there's nothing left of the target except some greyish ash on the ground.

When I hit William, he looks almost pitiful. I'm sure that if he had a few moments he'd try to wheedle out of his predicament. Fortunately, it's too late for that. He grabs at his midsection (which clearly isn't there anymore) and watches horrorstruck as the terrible glow spreads outward to his extremities. The last I see of him is his long, tapered fingers (perfect for sleight of hand, I think admiringly) wiggling pathetically in the air. Then he is all gone.

"So much for Bad William," I sigh. I turn to look at Tam, who has knelt beside me during the whole battle, keeping William at bay. But she has collapsed to the floor, her face flushed and sweaty.

The knights freeze in their tracks.

"Palina," I call. "Come over here . . . Tam has collapsed."

Palina rushes to her sister's side and cradles her head in her lap. Just a kid, I think, but she's the real hero.

Palina is giving her a sip of some Nevian medical liquor when Rufo comes up and slaps me on the back. "Don't worry, Alex, Tam is tough. The strain was a lot for her, but she'll be fine, won't she, Palina?"

"I . . . I don't know. She's not coming around. Maybe William attacked her inside . . . inside." She starts to cry.

Ineffectual as ever, I crouch down close to them. Tam is breathing, but it's a shallow, desperate wheeze. Palina leans into me. Rufo undoes all his weaponry and searches in his pack for something.

"I have some Nevian stimulants," he mutters. "They'll bring her around, they'll . . ."

But Palina just shakes her head. "No . . ." she moans. "It's her mind, her will, it's been wounded. She's got to fight her way back to consciousness, back to this world—"

I run my hand along Tam's forehead, pushing the hair away from the sticky wet skin.

And she opens her eyes.

Palina is looking at her. "Is it over?" Tam says in a whisper.

Palina turns to her, squeals, and crushes her brave sister to her. "Tam, you're back . . . you're okay."

"Well, I wouldn't say okay," she smiles. "My

mouth feels like blindworms have been nesting in it. Anybody have some bubble gum?"

"A whole case for you, sprout, just as soon as we get off this crazy world," I grin.

We're rather rudely interrupted by the sound of two doors, off to the side, being roughly thrown open. A small squad of soldiers enters—humans, from the look of them. Rufo's hand goes to his sword, and I try to remember where I've put my gun.

Then they freeze in their tracks, staring at the forest of now-inactive construct-knights. "Where's William?" one of them demands.

Rufo stands up, his sword held out in front of him.

"He's dead," Rufo answers, gesturing at the small pile of ash. Palina is slowly getting her gun into firing position.

"You don't say," the leader grins, turning to the others. "Well, if that isn't the best news we've heard in years." He walks over to Bad William's greyish ashes.

"Dust thou art," I mumble.

"What's that?" Rufo asks.

"Nothing. Just a saying we have . . ."

The soldier comes over to us. "Gentlemen, the entire planet owes a great debt to you. Might we ask that one of you remain with us as an interim ruler until we can establish some kind of normal government?"

Everyone, of course, looks right at me.

"No way, gang. I did my job, and my administrative and financial abilities are nil. Just ask my ex-wife." I walk over to Rufo.

"On the other hand, Rufo here would be an almost perfect interim ruler, wouldn't that be true, Palina?"

Palina smiles and takes my hand. "Yes, Rufo, do say you'll do it. Just until the people can get on their feet again."

"But . . . but . . ." he stammers, "I left Regina and Mara back at my beach house on Eldon. They'll wonder . . ."

"You can always send for them, you horny old goat," Palina scolds. "It's for the good of the empire, and the empress would be most pleased."

"Don't bring up that old bag, she still owes me for—"

The soldiers step closer to Rufo. "Please, sir. Without some kind of leadership, some other madman will just move in to take control."

Rufo looks back and forth as if trying to figure out some honorable way to duck this obligation. "Th . . . well, okay. But only for a short time. I don't like spending too much time in any one universe."

"Hurrah," Tam says. "And I will come and visit you."

"And I won't," I say. "No offense, but I've seen about as much of this place as I want to. One suggestion though. Tear down the arena and put in a nice, old-fashioned baseball stadium."

Rufo laughs, while the guards buzz back and forth, asking each other, "What's baseball?"

"Now," I say to Palina, "if Tam is up to

traveling, there's a small matter of a million dollars."

The trip out of William's world is certainly easier than going in. It's sort of like taking the IRT from Flatbush, Brooklyn to Flushing, Queens—a lot of zigzagging back and forth, taking a gate from one universe to another.

Only one dicey moment, when we pass through a dismal corner of a Nevia valley, and these vampirelike birds start to swoop down on us, fangs bared and looking hungry. We dispatch a few of them and, like startled crows, they soar away in search of safer prey.

Tam bounces back quickly, regaining her normal color and spunk. By the time we make our first gate journey, she's back to being as loud and obnoxious as any other eleven-year-old.

(And don't get me wrong. I'll never, ever, forget what the little squirt did when we went mano-a-mano with Bad William.)

Palina and I don't say much, but the silence between us speaks volumes. With the danger gone, she softens, allowing me to pretend that I knew what I was doing. (Hey, I'm not fooled, but I like a fantasy as much as the next person.) Sometimes, when Tam skips ahead, Palina's hand snakes its way toward mine and we stroll along that way.)

Further intimacies, though, are definitely postponed until we arrive at our destination.

And that is Center.

* * *

Section 99

After all the rough terrain we've been through, I'm not quite prepared for the overwhelming splendor of this, the ruling planet of the Twenty (plus one) Universes.

At first glance, Center looks quite Earthlike, in a romanticized, too-beautiful way. Palina explains to me that climate control is total, and the actual environments on the planet were also designed and constructed. The palace of the empress we travel to (which turns out to be only one of many) is built on top of a gentle hill, surrounded by beautifully manicured woods right out of Winnie the Pooh. The building itself is a light, gracefully arching structure. No attempt has been made to blend it into the natural surroundings, but the beauty of the palace makes it a welcome addition.

Travel in Center is also easier. There's no need to tramp around, as pleasant a prospect as that might be. On Center, travel is carried out by means of apports, which act like mechanical gates. They're capable of shuttling people all over the planet. They use no "magic" (as I call it), but Palina is quick to remind me that what I call magic is simply a different kind of technology.

And I inevitably think of the aborigines who were visited by an airplane, and later built a stick and straw model—an idol to be worshiped as they awaited the return of the "god from the sky." One man's logic is someone else's engineering.

Our actual arrival into the palace couldn't be more splendid.

We arrive, courtesy of one of the apports, in a tremendous hall with a beveled glass roof that sends rainbow streaks of light criss crossing through the massive room. Music begins on cue as we enter. (I grab Palina's hand, more than overwhelmed by the beauty of it all.)

The assembled crowd (most of them people, but there are some guys who look like over-grown chinchillas and a few veritable lounge lizards smoking cigars) breaks into applause and then presses close.

"Try this, Alex. You look like you had a rough couple of days."

It's Oscar, handing me a thin, fluted glass filled with a pale blue liquid. "Well," I say, "it wasn't so bad. I just wish I hadn't had Palina and Tam slowing me down."

Palina shakes her head at my joke and then smiles.

"Mother," she says, looking past Oscar.

And there, next to Oscar, stands one of the most beautiful women I have ever seen. Her hair is long and flows in gentle waves below her shoulders. A crimson and gold dress seems glued to a body full of inviting curves and lines.

"So this is Alex Tanen, our hero."

Oscar can't help but notice my rapturous attention, but he grins good-naturedly.

"Alex, let me present the Empress of the Twenty Universes, my wife, Star."

Palina has briefed me on how to greet her mother.

"Your Wisdom," I say softly.

Section 99

Then she surprises me. She comes closer, really close so I smell her incredibly wonderful perfume. She kisses me.

"You must call me Star, Alex. After all, it is you who saved this world . . . and probably my life."

"I hear old Rufo elected to stay," Oscar says.

I finish the blue liquor and help myself to some steaming canapes that come floating by. "Drafted is a more accurate description. He was a good sport about it, though."

"Probably he's disappointed that he'll be separated from his wenches."

"Alex." It's Palina, gently pulling on my hand. "Will you dance with me?"

I excuse myself to Star and Oscar.

Dancing was never my strong point, but I brave the dance floor with Palina, letting her take the lead.

"What will you do now?" she asks, her lips close to me.

"Do? I imagine I'll go home. Unless Oscar dreams up another quest for me—which I certainly hope he doesn't. If I'm not wrong, there's a small matter of one million dollars to be dealt with."

She stops dancing. "Has that been all it's meant for you? All about money?"

"No, not at all. But I'm not about to forget it. A deal's a—"

But she storms away from me.

And just at that point, the music stops and Oscar is on a raised platform speaking about yours truly.

I won't bore you with the wonderful things he says about me. I do have *some* modesty. But even at my best magic performance (Vegas 1982, at the Sands) I never received such an ovation.

"Finally," Oscar says, holding a small satchel aloft, "as a token of our gratitude, we would like to present Alex Tanen with a million Earth dollars and, of course, a return trip home."

More thunderous applause, and Oscar signals me to come close to him. (I wonder why there's a twinkle in his eye.)

I step up to him. Oscar speaks softly.

"You can take the money, pal. Or maybe you'd be more interested in other options."

What's this, I think. Let's make a deal? I wait.

"You could stay here, Alex. Live among us. Be sort of a 'court magician.' We might need your special talents in the future. Plus I can always use someone I can trust. I'd like you to stay."

Star has been sitting, and she stands and places a hand on my arm. "And I'd like you to stay."

Oscar makes a small tilt with his head. "And you know *she'd* like you to stay." Palina is standing near the back, talking to someone and trying to take no notice of my little awards ceremony.

"But you have to decide now. There's a convenient gate opening to Earth today."

I look at Palina. I look at the money.

"I could come back if I left, couldn't I?"

Section 99

Oscar's face clouds. "Perhaps. There's a difficulty with bringing people back and forth from one universe to another. Our scientists are concerned by what its effects may be on Earth history.

"So what will it be, Alex? Our home . . . or yours?"

Roll 3 D6.

If the total is less than or equal to Alex's value for Wisdom, turn to section 98.

If the total is greater than Alex's value for Wisdom, turn to section 101.

* **100** *

Here's the long and short of it.

Palina and I got married (by the empress herself, no less) and Palina (whose financial resources, it turns out, would make the Hunt brothers choke) set us up with a couple of houses in various universes. The one I like best is a three-story townhouse right on a secluded beach. (It's nice and quiet, except when Tam visits.) Our neighbors are Star and Oscar, and we have the crystal blue waves to ourselves. It's an absolutely wonderful place to live.

But even moonlight skinny-dipping à quatre can get boring, and Palina and I also live in one of Center's most elegant cities, a metal and glass jewel that, at night, sparkles like a tiara.

We had one child—a girl we named Elena— and later on a noisy boy whom, much to Oscar's chagrin, I call Gordon.

And did I forget about my magic? Not at all. In fact, I've begun to master the "advanced technology" of Center and mix in some sleight of hand stuff that surprises and shocks even Star's normally jaded constituency.

And yes, there was another time that Oscar

and Star had need of my services. It was even more dangerous than our little jaunt to Bad William's.

Fate, it turned out, had one more trick to play.

But that's a tale for another time.

THE END

* **101** *

I don't belong here, I think. Despite this wonderful planet, which looks like it was landscaped by Walt Disney, and the fabulous food, and the women who seem to be completely unabashed about exposing delicious parts of their bodies (as do the men, but I don't watch them), this isn't home.

My home is on Earth . . . and I'm a stage magician, trooping from show to show, plying the noble art of illusion.

I look at Palina. Tam is beside her, and they both seem to be avoiding me, as if they are aware that I might be leaving them.

"I've made my decision, Easy Gordon."

If Alex stays, turn to section 100.

If Alex leaves and returns to Earth, turn to section 103.

* 102 *

A knight comes staggering toward me, and neither Rufo nor Palina is there to protect me.

Some hero, I think.

"Keep firing," Tam orders. "I can't hold him for much longer."

The knight raises his sword to swing at me. "Do you mind if I dodge the knife?" I ask Tam.

The knight starts slashing the air.

KNIGHT
To hit Alex: 8
Damage: 1 D6 +1
The knight gets to attack before Alex shoots again.

If Alex has no hit points left, turn to section 29.
Otherwise, roll 3 D6.
Alex will hit William if he rolls 10 or less.

If he does so, turn to section 99.
If he misses, the knight attacks again. Continue the battle until either William is hit or Alex is out of hit points.

∗ **103** ∗

I tell them that Earth is my home and I want to
return. I can see that my decision is causing
more than mild disappointment. Star leaves
the podium immediately, and Oscar hands me
the money, the smile gone from his face.

"Come, Alex, we must get moving."

"I want to see Palina . . . to say . . ."

But she has left the room, vanished into the
vastness of the palace. Oscar is walking away
and I follow, the bag of loot dangling from my
hand.

It's no fun feeling venal.

Months later, I'm performing at Feldman's
—a Catskills resort that features second-
drawer performers that sing, dance, make
jokes while the patrons wolf down a cuisine
replete with starches, carbohydrates, fats, and
sweets. At one stage I think I can almost hear
the buttons struggling to pop off their bursting
bellies.

Most of my money is invested in a nice
assortment of blue-chip stocks and bonds. (I
did buy, I have to admit, a 1959 Corvette—

you know, like the one on *Route 66*. Two-toned, wire wheels, and with an engine in immaculate condition.

I can tell my story to no one. I've been warned by Oscar that only bad things will happen if I speak of the Twenty Universes, the gates, and all that. But, besides that, I know that no one would believe me anyway.

The sad part is that I didn't immediately realize I'd made the wrong decision. My little bag of money helps me forget Palina. Now, I pine away for her like a love-sick teenager. Only there's no way to contact Oscar, to beg, plead, please, please let me change my mind.

So I go on performing, somehow a bit bored with my home planet.

I'm nearly done with my act at Feldman's (another lackluster performance accompanied by blatant indifference) when I ask for a volunteer from the audience. And he stands up. All seven feet of him. He starts moving right toward me.

"A construct," I whisper, not believing what I'm seeing.

It's holding one of those steak knives from the table and making right for me.

"Sir, perhaps you'd like to take your seat," I say.

The audience, though, is screaming and moving their chairs away from the monster.

I try to run. Then, there is another one in the wings, also coming toward me.

Aren't I lucky?

"Hey," I yell to them, "I'm out of the hero business."

"That's what you think, Alex, my lad." Rufo comes barreling in from the back. (Literally— he knocks over about half a dozen overstuffed diners.)

"Rufo!" I shout. And I watch with admiration as he neatly slashes one of the constructs in two.

"Duck!" someone yells. A sweet voice that I know—and I'm in heaven.

I duck and turn to see Palina neatly skewer the other construct. Then she runs up to me and takes my hand.

"C'mon, Alex, my love, your friend Oscar has need of you."

"And I need you, Palina."

"Aren't you sweet, Alex," she says, and she gives me a quick kiss.

"If you two lovebirds don't mind, we have to get moving."

Palina pulls me up to a standing position.

"Ready to come with us?"

I nod to Palina.

"You'll have to leave your money."

I smile. A fool in love.

"What's a million bucks?" I say.

She grins and leads me to the front door, toward Rufo, who is already running to a gate, and another adventure in the Twenty Universes.

THE END